Juan Antonio rounded the back of the plane to greet the new man.

"Oh, Lord," he groaned. "Say it's not so. Oh please, say it's not so."

"Who are you?" He ground out the words. His hands fastened tightly around arms that couldn't possibly belong to a man. In one swift movement he pulled the scrawny youth to his feet. Green eyes peered owlishly at him through wisps of hair that escaped from a precariously hanging clasp. The youth extended his right hand.

"Carina Garza, the fruit inspector."

A roar started in his ears; a haze slowly covered his eyes. This could not be happening. A mistake, a horrible mistake had been made. With the palm of his hand he smacked the side of the plane.

"Get back on that plane," he growled through gritted teeth. "No woman is going to tell me how to run my plantation."

He had to get out of here before he did something stupid. Turning, he hurried to his vehicle, unaware that he'd given the pilot the "all clear for takeoff" signal, and that as he spurred the Suburban along the track to the hacienda, the plane lifted off the runway in the opposite direction, leaving the woman standing in the middle of nowhere.

JEAN KINCAID

and her husband, Dale, are missionaries to the Hispanic people in Old Mexico and the Rio Grande Valley. Her husband pastors Cornerstone Baptist Church in Donna, Texas, where Jean teaches the junior girls' class and sings in the rondalla. They have three adult children and twelve grandchildren. Jean speaks at ladies' retreats and women's events, and enjoys all things mission related. Her favorite time of day is early morning, when she spends time in devotional reading and prayer. Her heart's desire is to create stories that will draw people to a saving knowledge of our Lord Jesus Christ. You may contact her at www.jeankincaid.com.

JEAN KINCAID

The Marriage Ultimatum

HEARTSONG
PRESENTS

Recycling programs for this product may not exist in your area.

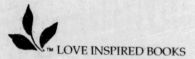

™ LOVE INSPIRED BOOKS

ISBN-13: 978-0-373-48667-0

THE MARRIAGE ULTIMATUM

Copyright © 2013 by Jean Kincaid

Printed in U.S.A.

There is no fear in love;
but perfect love casteth out fear:
because fear hath torment.
He that feareth is not made perfect in love.
—*1 John* 4:18

This book is dedicated to my husband, Dale Kincaid, for his patience and the many meals he supplied during the writing and editing process. Also to my editor, Kathy Davis, for encouraging, and believing in this story and for her love of all things Spanish. Last and most important, to my Savior for his fellowship and daily provision.

Chapter 1

Finally!

Juan Antonio's whole demeanor tautened. He peered across the study, head cocked sideways, listening intently for the slight sound that had snagged his attention. His hearing hadn't deceived him. The small Cessna airplane steadily approached then circled overhead twice before heading south to the dirt landing strip. "Buzzing" the house, it signaled the arrival of a guest or cargo that must be collected by someone from the plantation, namely himself. No cargo today, just one long-awaited fruit inspector. Surely this man would be better than the last one. He would have to be; he couldn't be worse.

Juan stood up, pushed his hands deep into his pockets and pulled out the keys to the Suburban. He lightly tossed them from one hand to the other, placed his chair under the desk and exited the house.

The last agricultural inspector sent to Mexico from the United States had been a grossly overweight, red-headed, fair-skinned man with a goatee. He'd complained about all the walking required for the job, been hospitalized for intense sunburn and had caught his goatee in the rollers on the packaging machine. Quick thinking on the part of the line boss prevented the inspector from being decapitated. *Ai caramba!* Juan Antonio had been happy to see the backside of the man as he boarded the airplane on his way out of the country.

However, the lack of a fruit inspector on a mango plantation equaled lost time, wages, profit—and rotten fruit. Without a good harvest, he'd never sell this property for its true value, effectively ending his dream of starting his own ranch in Texas.

From habit, Juan Antonio checked the road both ways upon leaving the main drive to the hacienda. His land encompassed over fifteen hundred acres, and though he seldom met regular traffic, there was always the chance of tractors, cultivators and other heavy equipment zipping in and out the rows onto the gravel driveway that wound through his land down to the airstrip, a couple of miles away.

Tightening his grip on the steering wheel, he winged a few words heavenward. "Lord, You gotta' make this work out. My dreams and ambitions are dependent on this inspection. I just simply cannot take any more disappointments." That God wasn't listening vaguely crossed his mind. Just how long it'd been since he had last spoken with Him didn't bode well for speedy delivery help from above.

He parked the Chevy Suburban to the left of the plane and hurried to help unload the luggage. The in-

stacked her luggage together and pulled the heavy load behind her down the track.

"The jerk! How could he just drive off and leave me?" Carina grabbed for the smaller suitcase before it finished its sudden slide to the ground. Realizing it wasn't going to stay put, she slung the strap over her shoulder, grabbed the handle of the wheeled suitcase and started off again.

"I should have taken that self-defense course the school offered," she muttered. "How I'd love to pull a stunt like that little Chinese man in the movies. Eeeeee-yiiiiii, and a quick jab to the solar plexus. Then, when he doubled over, I could whack him on the back of the head. He'd be on his knees begging for mercy." Satisfaction gleamed in her eyes. "'No woman's gonna tell me how to run my plantation!'" she mocked. Boy, did he ever remind her of somebody. At the moment it eluded her as to who it was.

A fly buzzed around her head and she swatted at it. Sweat beaded on her forehead and trickled down her face and neck. The sun sat mercilessly overhead, its rays burning the exposed skin on her arms. She stopped, opened the smaller suitcase and rummaged inside. Slipping on a long-sleeved shirt, she then sought for something to shield her face from the sun's rays. *Well, desperate times call for desperate measures,* she thought. She took another long-sleeved shirt from her clothing, stood up straight, placed her agricultural manual on her head with the shirt over it and tied the sleeves under her chin. Unable to move her head in any direction lest the contraption fall, she bent at the knees, eyes straight ahead. She groped around till she found the handle of her luggage, carefully straightened and marched off. A low chuckle escaped. She recalled how her kindergarten teacher, Mrs. Badillo, lined the class up for the bathroom break and singsonged, "Eyes forward." She and her classmates marched, much as she did now, with heads straight and eyes looking forward. God must have a sense of humor if He'd started preparing her for this moment seventeen years ago.

She glanced at her watch. "Oh, great. Siesta time. Not a soul's gonna be stirring for two hours or more." Hearing the whine in her voice, she gritted her teeth and trudged on.

In the airplane, they'd circled the hacienda twice before landing. The pilot informed her that this signaled to anyone in the house or fields that someone needed to meet the plane for news, visitors or cargo. Just seconds after compassing the house, they'd arrived at the airstrip, so according to her calculations, a thirty-minute hike seemed reasonable.

Forty minutes later, surrounded by stalks of corn higher than her head, doubts arose in multiples. She wasn't afraid, really. Was she? She spoke perfect Spanish. She could explain what she was doing here. "Oh, *sí, señor.* I am out for a stroll in the hottest part of the day. No, no, don't believe in siestas. I'd rather get heatstroke and die." Sarcasm dripped between huffed breaths as she hurriedly walked the never-ending row. "What's with the corn?" she grumbled. "This is supposed to be a mango plantation."

Finally she came to the end of the row and the slow burn returned with a vengeance. The black Suburban sat a hundred yards or so in front of her. Beyond the vehicle, bright red bougainvillea crept up the side of a white stucco villa. She rounded the front of the vehicle full steam ahead.

Chapter 2

"No, no!" Juan Antonio jabbed a finger in the air for emphasis. "Do not put me on hold. I am calling from… *¡Ay, caramba!* Crazy woman." He switched the phone to his other ear. "I cannot believe she put me on hold."

"Señor Fuentes?" The disembodied voice of a man came through the telephone.

"Yes, yes, it is I," he hastened to assure the man.

"What can we do for you today?"

"Oh, surely I do not have to start this conversation all over again?" he asked incredulously. "I have been on this phone for the past thirty minutes explaining what you can do for me. I asked you to send an inspector here *pronto,* and what did you do? You sent me a child. A woman child."

"I assume you are speaking of Ms. Garza, is that

correct?" The calmness in the voice served only to infuriate Juan Antonio further.

"I assume you could be right, although I don't rightly remember her name. You assured me that you'd send the best this time, so we could complete harvesting on schedule. Now we will fall behind even more *y es la culpa de ustedes.*"

"Señor Fuentes, it will not be our fault." The voice interpreted Juan Antonio's Spanish. "And we sent you our best. Ms. Garza graduated top in her class with honors. She has proven to be one of the greatest field reps in the Texas division."

"But she is a woman!" The words exploded from him.

"Yes, she is," the voice soothed insincerely.

"Well, that will not do." Juan Antonio's voice rang with command.

"Señor Fuentes?"

"Yes?"

"You need an inspector. We sent you the best that we have. Has Ms. Garza done something to displease you?" the courteous voice inquired in a patronizing tone.

Juan Antonio sighed with exasperation. He struggled to control the anger and helplessness pulsing through him.

"You do *not* understand, sir. Mexico is a man's world. Never in a million years will the men permit a woman to inspect their orchards. This Garza child, woman," he stammered, "whatever she is, is of absolutely no use to us. You must send someone else, and it needs to be…"

Juan Antonio faltered, interrupted by pounding on the back door of the hacienda.

"Señor Fuentes, Ms. Garza will take charge of this

operation as planned," the voice announced with quiet firmness, "or your co-op will lose its contract with NAFTA. Our male personnel are unavailable and she is the top agriculture inspector." *So that's that,* the voice seemed to say.

"But once again, you don't understand," Juan Antonio began, but the banging on the door increased, with what sounded like an occasional kick thrown in. "I, ah…" Juan Antonio watched as the door handle twisted back and forth. The lock held. "*Bueno.* I'll talk to you later." He placed the phone on the hook, effectively cutting off the voice of reason on the other end. Someone wanted in his house and they weren't being very nice about it. With long purposeful strides he reached the door and pulled it open.

The woman child stood in front of him pulling frantically at a flat contraption that oddly enough looked like a book covered with a shirt tied by the sleeves under her chin. The book had slipped down over her face and wedged under her chin, covering half her face, yet the top of the shirt held tight around the back of her head.

"What the…"

She froze at the sound of his voice.

He reached out and pulled upward on the book, effectively freeing her from bondage. And they wanted him to believe she graduated top of her class with honors?

Aye yai yai, Carina silently groaned. *Must I always look like a fool in front of him?* Squaring her shoulders, she stared him straight in the eye and said the first thing that came to mind. "Forget something back at the runway?"

To her horror, she watched amusement tilt the corners of his mouth.

She lifted a finger and poked him hard in the chest. "Bad move."

"Ow!" he yelped.

She brushed by him, gaining pleasure from the *whack, thump* of the suitcase that banged his legs as she passed.

Whirling back around, ready to give him a piece of her mind she saw that he massaged the place where she had jabbed him.

"Oh, that's mild compared to what I'd like to do to you," she lashed out. Her pride had been seriously bruised by his behavior, and she fought against the unfamiliar sense of defeat.

Her misery was so acute she knew tears were just a blink away, but she would eat glass before she'd allow him to see that weakness.

"Where is my room?" she demanded, but the quiver in her voice destroyed the effect.

Through the entire spectacle, he had studied her intently. Now, his hand swept out to the side. In an odd, yet gentle tone he spoke.

"I'm sorry. I…"

"No, no." Carina shook her head, a strong suggestion of reproach in her voice. "May I please just go to my room?"

He walked forward and stopped in front of her. Gently, he withdrew the strap of the carry-on from her shoulder, and placed it on his. Leaning toward her, his face just inches away, he reached behind her and nudged her hand from the handle of the suitcase. With a sideways tip of his head, he motioned to her. By tacit consent, they both turned and walked to the stairway.

Upstairs she watched him set her luggage inside the door of a bedroom and retreat downstairs as quickly as his legs would carry him. He seemed to instinctively know she had reached the end of her rope.

Juan Antonio climbed the stairs, the condensation from the glass of lemonade he carried trickling in little droplets down his hand. To his annoyance, guilt and confusion welded together in an upsurge of emotion. He thought she'd gotten back in the plane. *But you didn't check to be sure,* his conscience accused. And why, he questioned, had he felt himself responding to the vulnerability in her voice while she raged at him?

"*¡Ay, caramba!*" he whispered.

Anxious to escape his disturbing thoughts, he lifted his hand to knock on her door. Warning bells rang in his head and he caught hold of the door frame, straining to hear a sound that made him pause.

Over the noise of the shower, he distinguished an occasional sob, and exasperation mingled with guilt deep inside him. Trust a woman to cry over a little thing like being left at a runway. *She had to walk, you* idiota, *alone, in a strange place, during the heat of the day.* Surely, though, she'd faced a few hardships in her life; after all, she worked a man's job.

He descended the stairs on leaden feet, dumped the lemonade into the sink, then paced the kitchen in lonely silence.

Gradually, the knowledge of what he must do settled like a rock inside him and he planned his moves, down to the last detail.

* * *

Carina took her time getting dressed, in no hurry to face the man responsible for the crying jag she'd caved in to in the shower. Once she'd cried herself out, her strength revived and the hurt and embarrassment lessened.

So she'd had a bad start the first day on a new job. Wasn't that pretty much the norm? *I can do all things through Christ which strengtheneth me.* Philippians 4:13, the verse she'd clung to in college, ministered to her until confidence returned and with it a sense of renewal. She left the room with an air of calm composure and determination.

"I'm sorry." Juan Antonio greeted her with the apology as she stepped off the bottom stair. He looked as if he'd raked his hands through his hair a number of times. "I can't believe I acted in such a boorish manner. I wasn't prepared for the, um, uh, the upset you brought."

She widened her eyes in surprise. "Whatever did I do to upset you?" Carina enjoyed his struggle to recapture his composure.

"Hmm, you did that the minute I lifted you from the ground," he muttered. He guided her to the living room, his hand a soft touch on her back.

She sank to the sofa. His dark eyes gazed at her as if he would say something more, so she waited.

"Well?" she inquired softly.

The smile quickly faded from his face. He turned his back to her and crossed the room.

"Miss Garza…"

"Carina," she offered promptly.

"Carina," he responded, turning. "Please accept my apologies and let's just leave it at that, okay?"

Carina studied the man in front of her. For sure she'd never seen a more magnificent specimen of a man. From the black compelling eyes to the confident set of his shoulders, he radiated power. His lips were firm and sensual and the set of his chin suggested a stubborn streak. His hair was black, silky and straight. Caught off guard at her response to his good looks she lassoed her thoughts in a snap.

"I really would like it if you'd speak your mind. If we're going to be working together and living under the same roof, we should keep the air cleared, don't you think?"

"Oh, Ms. Garza, Carina. We will be doing nothing of the sort." He spun and walked from the room.

"Oh, no, you don't." Carina stalked after him. The man was making a habit of walking away from her.

Señor Fuentes stood behind an enormous old-fashioned desk, in a room that apparently served as his office and study. His presence dominated it, and she fought the dynamic vitality he exuded. She couldn't afford to be distracted by good looks, brawn or charisma.

"Please explain your last comment," she ordered in an authoritative voice.

"You and I, we will not work together. Tomorrow you will get on the plane and return to wherever you came from. Understand?"

She placed her hands on the desk opposite him and spoke slowly and distinctly.

"No, I do not understand. I have a contract. You have already promised your hospitality to my superiors. You need me here. The other plantation owners, they are expecting me."

He quickly rounded the desk toward her. Turning to

face him she gasped as he abruptly caught her by the elbows, pulling her hard up against him.

"Need?" His mouth twisted. "There is only one thing I would *need* you for, Ms. Garza, and I assure you it has nothing to do with mangos."

She yanked away from him. Dropping into the nearest chair she placed her hand over her heart in a futile attempt to drown out the loud thudding. She should be afraid, but wasn't. What a sorry, low-down trick to pull. How chauvinistic! How could he sink so low! She made a quick involuntary appraisal of his features.

He'd retreated and sat on the edge of his desk. His black eyes pierced the distance between them.

"Now you begin to get the picture, eh? You think I'm the only ogre out there that would think these thoughts? Why would your parents permit you to enter a man's work field? Can't they see the dangers of a woman alone on the plantation, working with the men? No? Then that's too bad because I—" he pointed to his chest "—I, Señor Juan Antonio Fuentes, will not allow it."

Lord, give me strength! This man was in dire need of an attitude adjustment toward women.

"And just what dream world do you live in to assume I would sit idly by and let you ruin my life like that? My career? I worked hard for a degree in agriculture. I love this job. Not every man behaves as you just did."

Carina's stomach lurched, and feeling a little sick she glanced away. "Please." Her voice shook. "May I use your bathroom?"

Juan Antonio strode across the room and opened another door. He spoke with a touch of grimness. "The lavatory is along the hall, first door on the left. You will find everything you need."

She strode into the bathroom, and finally alone, she slid down the closed door, and hugged her legs to her chest. The cold from the tiles seeped slowly into her and still she sat, head resting tiredly on her knees. Would it ever end? How long must she fight for her right to do the job she had trained to do?

She came here to work. Partial payment for her services now lay secure in her bank account. People depended on her. The other agents in her outfit were already working in assigned positions. Juan Antonio needed to be assured that she could do the job. No one else was available. She would have to do the convincing.

"Carina? *¿Estás bien?*"

Carina couldn't stop the sardonic smile that tipped the corners of her mouth. Juan Antonio's lapse into Spanish reminded her so much of her dad. Whenever *Papi* patronized a member of their family, he spoke Spanish because he had a better grasp of that language and appeared more forceful, more in control. He expected his suggestions to be adhered to no matter what his wife or children wanted. Well, she'd had enough of that to last her a lifetime.

"Yes, I'm fine. I'll be right out." She reached for the door handle and pulled herself up. She crossed to the ceramic sink and ran cold water through shaky hands and touched her face. She dried her hands then fluffed her hair. *Well, Mr. Fuentes. You are in for a fight.* Her stomach growled. *But right now, I need food and you're going to feed me.*

As she exited the bathroom Juan Antonio led her through to a small room off the *sala*. By the window stood a table, covered with an immaculate red cloth, set with silverware and glasses of lemonade. He seated her just as a Spanish version of Aunt Bee entered the room. Juan Antonio introduced her as Alejandra, his housekeeper.

"*Hola,* Señora Alejandra." Carina's correct pronunciation of the housekeeper's name pleased her and it showed in the beaming face she turned in Carina's direction.

"*Mucho gusto, señorita.*"

"*Igualemente.* I am pleased to meet you, too."

Alejandra set a small bowl of *pico de gallo* on the table, a mixture Carina could make with her eyes closed. Chopped onion, cilantro, tomato and jalapeno, with lemon juice and a dash of salt. A metal ring held two smaller bowls, one with *salsa verde,* green salsa, created with the smaller, hotter peppers. The other contained red salsa made from tomatoes and garlic. From the smell of the *salsa verde,* it would burn the hair off your tongue.

Next the housekeeper removed two silver tops from plates she placed in front of Juan Antonio and Carina. Chile relleno, similar to a bell pepper, stuffed with white cheese, chicken, shrimp or beef, alongside rice and beans.

Carina cut into her pepper, the outside skin cooked so tender it gave way and steam rose from inside carrying with it the strong smell of oregano.

"Mmm, *señora,* this smells heavenly."

"*Muchas gracias,* Señorita Garza. *Total es bien?*"

"*Sí,* Alejandra," Juan Antonio answered. "Everything's fine."

"*Entonces, buen provecho.*"

"I'm sure we will enjoy this meal." Carina smiled at

the housekeeper and took her first bite. "Oh, yes, this is good," she murmured. "Just like Mother makes."

"You mo'ther, she cooks the Mexican deeches?"

Carina smiled at Alejandra's broken English.

"Yes, all the time. My mother is Hispanic. So was my father. In the last couple of years she's learned to cook American, but when my brothers and I were children she always cooked Mexican."

"*Perdon, señorita,* but you look so *gringa.*"

Carina watched Alejandra duck her head in embarrassment. To speak so boldly to a guest was considered rude by the older generation and it was plain to see that Alejandra thought she'd overstepped the bounds of courtesy.

Carina hastened to reassure her.

"It's okay. I am light-skinned, but by the time…"

"Alejandra, if we need something more, we will call you, *estas bien?*" Juan Antonio dismissed the housekeeper in a gentle voice.

"*Sí,* Señor Fuentes." The housekeeper gathered her tray and quickly left through a swinging door that led to the kitchen.

Carina sampled everything on her plate. She talked with Juan Antonio at length about the co-op, where the shipping plants were located, and the landowners involved. He questioned her about family, college and her degree. Alejandra came and cleared the table, yet still they sat, sipping coffee, easily conversing as if they'd been friends for a long time. Carina finished her drink and gathered the cups to carry them through to the kitchen.

"No. Ale will do that." Juan Antonio wiped his mouth with a white linen napkin and stood. "Come,

Carina. There is something you must do before you fall asleep on your feet."

"I am so sorry." She pressed a hand over her mouth as a second yawn caught her off guard. "I can't believe I'm so tired."

Carina followed him into the study and leaned wearily against the desk as Juan Antonio extracted paper and pen from the drawer.

"What is so important that we must do it now, Juan Antonio? I need sleep. I have a job to go to tomorrow." Hand to mouth, Carina quickly stifled another huge yawn.

"You had a job," he corrected. "If you will write out your resignation, I will see that it's delivered in the morning."

Carina looked warily at the pen Juan Antonio held out to her. Last night's sleep had been interrupted periodically with anticipation of this first day on the job. Now this unexpected ambush, combined with the previous events of the day, caused weakness to overwhelm her. She closed her eyes, grasping for inner stamina to strengthen her resolve. Surely he did not expect her to give up so easily. *You had a job, you had a job, you had a job,* whirled senselessly round and round in her mind. She sensed a blur of shaded light, then total darkness, and she was sinking, sinking…

Strong arms caught her up, so that she didn't feel the rising floor. Dimly she was aware of a soft mattress beneath her. A woman's voice spoke soothingly. "Rest easy, little one. All will be well."

Chapter 3

As Carina's head fell, helpless against his shoulder, Juan Antonio clicked his tongue reprovingly. Silly woman. He'd noticed earlier the exhaustion that lined her face, a combination, he felt sure, of too much sun and excitement and not enough water or rest. However, her eyes gleamed like summer lightning as she spoke of her life and family.

His gaze slid slowly over Carina's unresponsive figure cradled in his arms. Black lashes swept down across high cheekbones; her lips were full and rounded. *For certain* she was a beauty. He felt his defenses weakening. His heart swelled with a feeling he'd thought long since dead. *Why does she do this type of work? Is she from a family of poverty? She carries herself confidently, her proud shoulders erect.*

A frown wrinkled his brow and he hardened his heart

against any compassion awakening for this woman. He'd determined one thing for certain as she'd talked during their meal. She and his mother had much in common. They were both career-driven. Unable to give themselves completely to a man because of marriage to a job. He was sure of this.

"Ale," he spoke softly to the woman approaching him from the stairs. "Prepare Miss Garza's bed, *pronto.*"

"Sí, señor. ¿Que pasa con la señorita?" she questioned as she turned and started back up the stairs.

"I don't know what happened to the *señorita,*" he grumbled, unwilling to examine the fierce feelings of protectiveness coursing through him. "She seems to have passed out. *En realidad,* I think she's asleep."

"Pobrecita."

Juan Antonio waited as Alejandra pulled back the covers on the bed then moved aside so he could relinquish his burden.

"Poor child" indeed. Carina had only one person to blame for her condition. Herself! He found it vaguely disturbing that he felt so guilty, though.

Carina's head rolled wearily to the side as he lay her down. He grimaced as Alejandra smoothed the hair from her brow, all while whispering words of tenderness close to her ear. It was evident the beautiful wildcat touched the tender heart of his housekeeper. Well, that was just too bad.

Carina awakened the next morning, refreshed and anxious to begin the day. That something wasn't quite right became increasingly clear as the morning wore on. The housekeeper entered her room and spoke to her in hushed tones as if afraid of waking someone.

"Miss Carina, here is your breakfast. Would you like for me to pour *café?*"

"Oh, Aie, you shouldn't have brought this up. I don't usually eat in the mornings. I'll grab a piece of toast should I want something. Please don't worry about me." Noticing the dismayed look on the woman's face, Carina hastened to reassure her. "However, that coffee smells divine and you have surely made my day." Extending her cup to be filled, she leaned forward and impulsively kissed Ale on the cheek. Uneasiness stirred in her as the maid refused to meet her eyes and began stuffing things back in the suitcase lying open on the bed.

"Oh, *mi hijita,* I am so sorry." As Ale spoke, her voice wavered.

"What is it, Ale?" Carina placed the coffee back on the tray and grasped the older woman's hands, her sense of disquiet increasing.

"Miss Carina, he...he... You—" Before the house-keeper's words stuttered to a stop, some sixth sense warned Carina they were no longer alone. She whirled around to face the intruder, nerves stretched taut.

"Buenos días, lovely ladies. And how are you this morning, Carina? Did you sleep well?" Juan Antonio swept into the room, clapped his hands together, not waiting for a reply. "Well, then, let's get this show on the road. What is it we Americans say? We're burning daylight." In a courteous gesture, he swept his hands in front of him, bowing slightly at the waist, permitting her to exit the room first.

Carina stepped forward eagerly, Juan Antonio's enthusiasm lighting a warm glow inside her.

The ride to the airstrip, as well as the flight, were accomplished in uncertain silence. Juan Antonio's plane was smaller than the one she'd arrived in yesterday, and much louder. They both wore headsets, which drowned out some of the noise as they talked sporadically. The slight hesitation in Juan Antonio's voice each time she broached one subject or another should have warned her, prepared her, but her mind refused to register the significance of this flight.

When the tower in Tepic instructed them to a holding pattern, comprehension dawned and Carina whirled in her seat. There in the back of the plane sat her luggage.

The full sense of his betrayal registered on her senses. A feeling of inadequacy swept over her. Why hadn't she caught on to what he'd planned?

"You're taking me back," she stated. She stared at his profile until he turned and their eyes met.

"It would never have worked."

"You never gave it a chance."

Regrets assailed her. Her first foreign field job and she'd failed. *But it wasn't my fault!*

The door on this plane was below the wings, so she exited easily and walked, head high, into the terminal. She didn't say goodbye, never looked back, just strolled to the taxi stand outside the airport. As she opened the door of the taxi, Juan Antonio handed her luggage to the driver.

"Carina…" She closed the door, effectively shutting out his voice and gave the name of the hotel to the driver.

At the hotel, she collapsed onto the bed, discouraged and defeated. She'd have to get a flight out tomorrow. She dreaded facing her employers. She drifted into sleep, her heart heavy.

* * *

After a nap she called the airline to book a flight, but try as she might, there were no flights out of Tepic till the end of the week. She considered her options. There were six other orchard growers in the co-op. Because the seventh had a bias against females did not mean the other six would. Carina found her courage and determination returning, and she girded herself with resolve. She would proceed with the assignment.

She contacted owner Don Diego Marin, the second appointment on her list of orchards to inspect, and informed him of her intention to begin the next day. Having that settled, she felt lighthearted and free to enjoy herself.

Armed with her camera and a bit of cash, she set out to tour the town of Tepic. Juan Antonio Fuentes would not stop her. She would swat him like a fly.

Minutes later Carina fingered a tri-colored wool blanket tossed haphazardly across a braided rope. One rope end looped and then was tied to a light pole; the other end was connected with the edge of the adjoining store roof. A slight breeze stirred the blankets, raising a familiar scent to tease at her memory. Wet hay. Yes, that was it. *Abuelo,* her grandfather, raised horses and Carina's favorite pastime as a child had been lying in the straw daydreaming, especially when it rained. One corner of the barn leaked, and the sweet odor of wet hay permeated the air. Carina buried her nose in the soft wool cloth for a second, eyes closed, sniffing appreciatively, enjoying her brief nostalgic thoughts.

The blankets afforded a small amount of shade for the tiny Mexican woman seated on the sidewalk begging. Carina pulled change from her pocket and dropped it into a box the lady held up to her. Immediately children surrounded her, their hands raised imploringly.

"Please lady, one nickel?"

"One nickel, lady?"

"Hey, pretty lady. One dollar, please."

Finger waving back and forth, Carina laughingly refused the impudent children her hard-earned money. "No, no, no," she chided. *"No tengo dinero."*

Tables arrayed with various crafts, jewelry, carved animals, name-brand watches and T-shirts lined the streets in front of each store. Tejano music blared from loud speakers, the accordion and mariachi horns creating a lively Hispanic atmosphere. A jewelry booth caught her attention and she moved on to sample the handiwork of talented craftsmen. These people were her Mexican kinsmen.

Her father, born and raised in Nuevo Progresso, a Mexico border town alongside the Rio Grande River, was taught like the children she just passed, to beg for money. Especially from the "gringos" or visiting Americans. At the end of the day all the kids met at the back of an alley and handed over the money to their *jefe,* or boss. The *jefe* then gave them a percentage which most of the kids took home to their mothers. It was an accepted practice in Mexico, but Carina's dad hated it. From the time he was a small child he vowed to become an American and live "the good life."

Now here she was in her dad's homeland. He would turn over in his grave. Yet she loved it. The poverty and beauty appealed to something deep inside her. Employed as a United States top agriculturalist aka "fruit inspector," her assignment was to spend the next six months traveling among the mango plantations under consignment by the United States. She would test the pesticides used, and check the groves, both young saplings and mature trees, for dangerous fruit molds. She'd then catalog and reject anything against U.S. regulations. An absolute peachy job with incredibly sweet people. God had granted her the desires of her heart. Well, almost.

All her life she'd lived with some form of prejudice due to the Mexican blood flowing through her veins. Even as an American, born and raised in the United States, her Hispanic heritage caused many hardships a child should never have to face. A hard pill to swallow at times.

But this! This thing with Juan Antonio brought back old fears and insecurities. He was of the same Mexican descent. In despair she faced the harsh realities of chauvinism he'd exhibited. In college, she'd experienced much the same thing, guys who thought she should be in another occupation. *Women belong in the home. You should be having babies.* Would it never end?

Hunger pangs gnawed at her stomach, startling her from her reverie. She searched the crowded street for a taco stand. One thing Texas lacked that Mexico had in abundance was the rotisserie taco stands situated every few yards or so on the city streets. Spotting one close by, she approached and ordered tacos in perfect Spanish.

"How many you want, lady?" The man smiled, so very proud of his broken English. Incredible how everyone recognized she was American. She bore the same skin tone as the Mexicans. Her heritage was the same. But her dress, the confident way she walked, even her hairstyle screamed American.

"Dame quatro, por favor." Four tacos would defi-

nitely satisfy her hunger. The small round corn tortillas held a minimal amount of meat. Carina filled them
with the *pico de gallo* offered in a small bowl on the
end of the stand.

"Ah, heaven." she murmured, tilting her head back
to keep the little flecks of meat from escaping as she
chewed hungrily. With a slightly chilled Coke she
washed the food down, amused that a deposit would
be returned when she handed them back the bottle. How
dated was that? Glass coke bottles requiring deposits,
still in use.

She wiped her mouth with a napkin, then retrieved
her deposit. As she sauntered back to the hotel, she
adopted the laid-back attitude of the native Mexicans.
Time seemed of no importance and the reminder of
Papa's constant prodding during her childhood faded
in the face of such relaxed conditions.

Chapter 4

Broken pavement made driving hazardous in Mexico and kept drivers attentive. Signs lined the roads with warnings of *Curvas Peligosa*. Dangerous curves seemed an understatement, and not just for vehicles. Señor Juan Antonio was certainly a dangerous curve that had wound round her. One couldn't predict what the next bend hid.

Carina automatically leaned to the right, grasping the back of the seat in front of her as the driver swung the bus sharply to the left, narrowly missing other vehicles exiting the road to San Blas. *Why didn't I rent a car? I could have been in San Blas an hour ago.* The receding blare of horns fed the aggravation wearing at her frayed nerves. She laid her head against the window, her mind congested with conflicting emotions.

Though her mind clamored, the world outside the

bus window began to intrude on her reflections. Sitting up straight on the bus seat, she stared through the window at the mango field they passed. The new *autopista* they traveled, built higher than the fields to prevent flooding, permitted perfect viewing over the tops of the trees. What had captured her attention? Yes, yes, there it was again. Carina narrowed her eyes against the sun as she examined the grove further. There. Though the mango trees formed one large foliage carpet due to their height and breadth, every now and then there was a gap, a space that wasn't supposed to be there. If she didn't miss her guess, a fungus had caused the brown, bare spots. One that would greatly affect the producing yields of this grove.

A driver met Carina at the bus stop and escorted her to the barns of the *Rancho de Diego*. She introduced herself as the new inspector to the owner, Don Diego Marin, and while he wasn't exactly welcoming, he refrained from pointing out the obvious, that she was a woman. Deciding to research the area thoroughly before confiding her suspicions to anyone, Carina happily bade Don Diego goodbye, and climbed on the mode of transportation at her disposal. She turned the key, pressed the gas and the golf cart effectively carried her to her destination. The middle of the mango grove.

Four hours and thirty-three minutes later, she gave the sad news to the Don. His orchard, while beautiful from the bottom, was sick with disease. Flower blight, fruit rot and leaf spots were among the few signs spotted by the naked eye. Carina shared the results of each test with Don Diego, explaining in detail the care needed to bring the orchard back to good health, keenly aware that the more she spoke the more incensed he became.

"Señor Diego, we will need to work on your mango grove for the next several weeks. Is there a place available for me to sleep while we decide our plan of action?"

"You are to live at the home of Juan Antonio Fuentes, are you not?" Don Diego regarded her with unfriendliness foreign to the majority of Mexican people.

"But I'll be spending my time here for quite a while. It would be easier to begin each day before the sun is up if I am housed close by." This guy didn't need to know what Juan Antonio had put her through. That high-profile rejection might affect everyone with whom she was to work. She waited anxiously while Don Diego considered her reasoning.

"Bien, bien. Vamos." His expression a mask of stone, Don Diego led her toward the barns.

When he left, after showing Carina her new quarters, she closed the door, grimacing in good humor. She'd been demoted from a suite in a fancy hacienda to a bunk room in a barn. Determined, she grimly set about cleaning the bedroom and bath she'd been assigned. As the sun set on the horizon her determination faltered, and she fought hard to keep the tears at bay. Her backpack held clean clothes and travel necessities, but the bulk of her belongings were at the hotel in Tepic. A lone towel hung on the rack in the bathroom and the sheets, washed earlier by hand, hung over the chair and desk, not completely dry. Though both rooms were clean, an occasional cockroach made its presence known by running across the floor or up the wall.

Carina sat gingerly on the bed, ready to spring up at the first sign of a bug of any species. She rifled through her purse and found a strawberry Creme Saver and a slightly melted Tootsie Roll.

"Mmm, dinner." Resolved not to visit the main house unless invited, Carina popped the candy into her mouth, enjoying the rich fruit flavor.

Oh, Juan Antonio, why did you have to be an egotistical, chauvinistic...

She jumped up from the bed and grabbed the sheets off the chair. Dry or not, she'd have to sleep sometime tonight, so she might as well make the bed. Moments later, trying to bathe in the trickle of water coming from the shower head, Carina began to wish the last forty-eight hours had never occurred.

She dodged a cockroach when she stepped from the shower, then hurriedly dressed, checking first for foreign critters that might have decided they'd found a new home. Just as she reclined on the bed, staring up at the dim light she refused to extinguish, a thud sounded at the back wall.

Carina sat up crossed-legged on the bed, listening intently. Another bang against the wall made dust and tiny bits of trash escape the roof and walls of the cement building. There was only one door, so if someone wanted in, why didn't they use it? Silence descended and for the next hour Carina lay alone with her thoughts.

On the edge between consciousness and dreamland she heard voices, murmuring and more hits on the wall.

"Hey," she yelled. "What are you doing out there?"

More muttering followed and then a bang so loud against the wall, Carina rushed to the door, yanked it open and crashed right into someone intent upon entering. She fell back against the opened door awkwardly, in a spiral slide to the floor. Hands grabbed her shoulders, halting her fall, one arm wrapping round the front of her, her back caught up against a hard chest. Sheer black fright swept through her. She fought like a wild-cat, yet the arm tightened, unyielding as a band of steel. She turned her head sideways and sank her teeth into the intruder's upper arm. He grunted in pain, then flung her writhing body forward and she landed on the bed hard, her breath almost leaving her. She doubled up for a Tae Bo kick but he caught both legs in an inflexible grip. She gasped, twisting and turning, a keen cry escaping her lips. "Oh, Lord, pleeeease help me."

"Carina, for Pete's sake. What is wrong with you?"

The fight went out of Carina's body, leaving her limp and weak. "Antonio?" she whispered.

"Yes, it's me. Open your eyes and see." His voice was smooth, but insistent.

Slowly she did as he asked and stared into beautiful coal-black midnight that blazed in anger. She didn't care. As he released her arms, she sprang from the bed and flung them around his neck.

"Oh thank you, thank you, thank you," she whispered fervently.

"Carina." He tried to ease her back but she latched on, hugging him even tighter.

Finally his arms wrapped around her like a warm blanket. The trembling began to subside as he kissed the side of her head, all while murmuring words of comfort.

"Shh, *chiquita. Estas bien.* You're safe. I'm here. Nothing will happen to you."

A long quiet moment slipped past as she relaxed against him. Content, she made a small sound of protest as he gently grasped her upper arms and held her away from him.

"Carina." His voice trailed off as she looked up at him, causing one lone tear to roll down her cheek.

"What happened that frightened you so?" Then as the anger returned, he shook her gently. "What are you doing here? I told you to go home. I flew you to Tepic myself. You can *not* work here." Each word was punctuated by a gentle shake, but before Carina could answer the doorway filled with Don Diego and several of his men.

"Aha, *señorita.* You misled me. If Juan Antonio dismissed you, then you should not have been working in our grove. That is trespassing. Perhaps the *Federales* would be interested in this information, eh?"

"Oh, yes, Don Diego, you'd like that, wouldn't you? Then no one would be here to see that..." Her accusing words were choked off as Juan Antonio pulled her toward the door.

"Don Diego, my deepest apologies. I should have notified the *aduanas* that Ms. Garza was no longer employed as the U.S. representative. I will escort her to the plane tomorrow, myself, and see to it that we have a new agriculturalist immediately." As Juan Antonio talked he cleared a path to the black Suburban parked about a hundred yards from Carina's doorway.

"But..." Carina stuttered.

"Carina," Juan Antonio cautioned through gritted teeth.

"Juan Antonio, you don't understand. He..." She twisted, straining to pull her arm from his grasp. Without missing a beat, he propelled her forward while calling goodbyes back over his shoulder. He opened the door to the vehicle, swooped her up in his arms and placed her in the seat. Before she could utter a word the door closed, the indignity of the act robbing her of speech. The laughter of the men echoed round her when he opened his door.

"Juan Antonio, you—"

"Callate!"

Carina fell back against the seat, stunned. *I know he didn't just tell me to shut up!*

Chapter 5

Carina examined her rioting emotions as she hung on to the seat of the jolting Suburban. She'd like to give him a piece of her mind but her relief at being rescued warred with anger. She was so thankful he arrived when he did. Instinct told her to work on damage control, pronto.

Seconds later they turned onto smooth pavement and raced into the darkness. She relaxed against the seat, casting a quick glance at Juan Antonio.

"Juan Antonio, I've never been so glad to see…"

"Do not speak to me at this moment, Carina. *Estamos?*"

"Would it matter if I said, no, I am *not* with you on this?"

"I don't want to hear your explanation, Carina." His voice was hoarse with anger. "I tell you to return to the USA, you don't listen. I tell you this is no job for a woman, you don't listen. I explain to you in all seriousness that this job is dangerous, but you refuse to listen. Now I don't wish to hear *your* explanations. *Comprende?*"

"Sí, comprende." Oh, yes, she understood. How often had her father overruled all dissimilar opinions in their family? His word was law. Even her macho brothers never disobeyed whatever order he issued, followed by either *estamos* or *comprende.* However, Juan Antonio wasn't her father. Neither was she a child in need of an authority figure.

Lack of motion alerted Carina they'd reached their destination. She glanced up sleepily and realized they were at the hacienda.

"You'll stay the night here and tomorrow we'll sort all this out, okay?" Juan Antonio took charge with quiet assurance.

"Yes, thank you." Carina preceded him into the house and headed straight for the study.

"Where are you going? It's late. I'm tired. I'd just like to turn in." His voice sounded resigned.

"So am I. Tired, that is." Carina lost her train of thought as she stared into his compelling black eyes. The shadow of his beard gave him a distinctive manly aura. "I need to send a quick email about the anthracnose to the Ag center. May I use your computer, please?"

His dark eyes searched her face.

"Anthracnose?"

"Yeah." Pensively, she stared back at him.

"At Don Diego's?"

"Yes."

"You have proof of this?" He said the words tentatively as if weighing the whole series of events that had unfolded since yesterday.

"Yes, the test results are in my backpack." Carina widened her eyes in horrified despair. "Oh, no," she cried. "My backpack is still in the bunk room."

The corner of Juan Antonio's mouth twisted with exasperation. "*Aye yai yai.* What next?"

"We have to go back and get it. It contains all my documentation." She watched him with acute anxiety.

"We're both too tired to make the long trip back there tonight." He walked to the desk and sank heavily into the chair. Slowly, he rubbed his hand over his eyes then down his face. The tense lines across his forehead remained.

"Come, Carina. Sit down. Tell me about this fungus you think you've found at Don Diego's. What are the symptoms and what test did you run?"

"I noticed dead areas as the bus passed the orchard. Then while among the trees I found black spots on the leaves. I wasn't able to test any fruit, but I'd bet a thousand to one that there is fruit rot, as well." Carina seated herself on the edge of the wingback chair facing the desk.

"Did you test the soil?"

"Yes. There was no sign of verticillium wilt."

"So, what's the prognosis for Don Diego's yield this year?"

"Possibly he'll lose the majority of his fruit. Once my report goes in, special operators will inspect each crate of mangos. With anthracnose, serious decay problems may occur in transit, at the market and after sale. If that becomes the case, the co-op will earn a bad name and your fruit will not be bought."

"*Sí, sí.* This I know. It will affect us all." Juan Antonio's vexation strained his voice. "What must be done?"

"We need to begin a diligent fungicide program immediately and continue until the pre-harvest waiting period is reached. Then a post-harvest treatment will be required." Carina sat in her chair, fingers entwined in her lap. "Don Diego's fruit needs to be separated from the rest of the co-op's yield."

"Yes, yes, and he will not like it one bit." His eyelids lowered and his expression closed, shielding his thoughts from her.

"Don't do that, please," she muttered hastily.

"Do what?" He glanced at her for clarity.

"Hide your thoughts from me. You do that often, you know. We were having a great discussion, then suddenly you shut me out."

"Maybe I'm protecting you, Carina. Would that be so bad?" His voice was calm, his gaze steady.

"No, that wouldn't be bad. But there is a difference between protection and bigotry."

"You will explain what you mean by bigotry, please."

"A person intolerant of new ideas. Prejudiced. One who holds fast to an opinion whether it is correct or not." Carina reeled off the definition from memory, having learned firsthand what bigotry meant.

"And so, Carina." Juan Antonio strode around the desk, clasped her arm, then walked with her to the stairway. "Have you decided which I am? Protector or bigot?"

"Well, sir. You display characteristics of both."

"Then I guess we will just have to sleep on it, won't we?" Juan Antonio stopped outside the door to Carina's room. "You'll be fine, alone tonight? Today's havoc will not disturb your sleep?" His questioning gaze traveled slowly over her face. Carina stood, pinned to the floor as his hand gently touched her forehead and swept her hair back. "Carina?"

"Oh, yes. Yes, of course I'll be fine." Carina spoke in a husky whisper, her mouth lifting in mute invitation.

Softly his breath fanned her face like a whisper, but he seemed to think twice about it and turned and strode down the hall.

"Juan Antonio," she called softly after him.

His steps slowed and she knew he heard.

"Why were you trying to enter the bunk room from the back tonight? Why didn't you look for the door first?"

"Perdon?" Juan Antonio paused in front of his bedroom door and stared back at her.

"Tonight. At the bunkhouse. Why were you beating on the back wall? You scared the daylights out of me."

Juan Antonio seemed frozen, as if pondering something, then said, "It's late, Carina. We'll talk about this in the morning, *sí? Buenos noches.*"

"Good night, Juan Antonio."

Carina entered her bedroom and fell on the bed stifling a groan in the pillow. *Be still, my beating heart.*

Juan Antonio grunted as he landed awkwardly on the other side of the fence. Running quickly to hide beneath the cover of the trees, he stealthily worked his way through the orchard toward the bunkhouse. *Crazy old man. How dare he scare a woman!* Juan Antonio felt the barely controlled anger coiled in his body. Tonight when Carina asked him why he hadn't just come to the door first, realization swept over him. Don Diego and his men had tried to frighten her off.

Earlier this evening, Juan Antonio, intent upon informing Don Diego that a different inspector would be arriving shortly, had gone to the hacienda first and been informed that Don Diego was at the bunkhouse. He'd lifted his hand to knock at the door when Carina came barreling out, slammed into him and fell. She'd fought like a tigress. But in his own conceit and anger at her disobedience, he'd forgotten that terror until she questioned him.

Oh, he was familiar with the technique. One carried over from the old school. They would scare her till she gave up and left, then sweep the information about the bad fruit under the rug, smiling the whole time they accepted payment from the Americans. Never looking to the future and the fact that once discovered, there would be no customers for their fruit. And, with total lack of regard for his neighbors who would suffer at this deceit. Once the bad fruit was discovered, the buyers would look for new growers. Juan Antonio couldn't let that happen. He needed a great harvest this season in order to expedite the sale of the hacienda.

Well, they'd crossed the line. They shouldn't have messed with a woman. He remembered her trembling in his arms as he assured her she was safe.

Hugging the shadows, he arrived at the bunkhouse. In a flash he entered, closing the door behind him. Quickly, he sank to his haunches and waited for its occupant to swing at his head, allowing him to launch a full-body attack to the midriff.

Not a sound. Nothing moved. Juan Antonio drew a matchbook from his pocket and lit a match, shaking it out quickly as he spotted the backpack lying on the floor by the bed. Snatching it up, he stood by the door listening, then exited the building, gliding into the night, cautiously observing each shadow, until he climbed the fence, started the Suburban and headed toward Tepic instead of the hacienda. Might as well finish everything tonight. Carina needed her things and he needed a housekeeper as a chaperone. This was going to be a long night.

Carina woke and stretched slowly under the cotton sheet that was her only covering. Gray light of dawn poured through the slats of the tall shuttered windows. The whirr of the ceiling fan, barely audible, gently moved the morning air over her. She listened intently, soaking up the alien sounds.

She sat up and drew her knees to her chin, shivering a little. A startled shriek broke from her lips as she spotted her luggage and backpack sitting just inside the door.

"Glory be, glory be." She jumped from the bed and ran to her belongings. "My clothes, my makeup," she cried. "Oh, happy day, deodorant."

The bathroom off her room was small but the hot water tempted her to linger. The smell of her bath gel and shampoo as she lathered up parted her lips in soundless delight.

She toweled down quickly, blow-drying her hair into soft, silken strands. Dressed in white Capri pants and a soft yellow shirt that tied at the waist, she searched through her luggage till she found the thong flip-flops that completed the outfit. A light makeup moisturizer, hurriedly applied, a quick dab of perfume and she was ready. The need to be out and about was much more pressing than her looks.

Her mind zipped and zinged over the significance of the luggage arrival. How had it gotten here and did its appearance mean she would be staying?

Moments later in the kitchen she glanced at her watch. Where was everybody? This was a working plantation, yet at eight-fifteen, no one stirred. No smell of coffee or bacon permeated the air. Juan Antonio most likely left for the orchards long before the sun touched the horizon, but where was Alejandra?

Carina wandered through the first floor of the hacienda in search of anyone who could tell her the plans for today. Encountering no one, she sighed and headed back to the kitchen.

Unlocking the arched wooden plank door, Carina slipped outside the house. To the right of her sat the black Suburban. She turned left and followed a path to the back of the house. She stared in awe at the jungle of rioting plants and bushes. Not one speck of grass grew among them and the packed dirt appeared to have been swept.

An intense longing to see her mother swept through her. Mother never allowed grass to grow among her flowers, either. She believed the grass took all the food from the soil.

Carina walked between the plants, touching this one, smelling the next. How could anyone see nature's beautiful handiwork and not comprehend that there was a God? Peace enveloped Carina and she hummed as she strolled along.

She wasn't sure of the moment when she knew she was being watched, but she felt the impact like a hand jostling her shoulder. She risked a swift look around, realizing belatedly she'd wandered quite a distance.

Observing nothing out of the ordinary, she casually turned and walked back toward the house. The unusual sensation remained and she glanced up to measure the distance between herself and the back door. Movement at a window on the second floor snared her attention.

Juan Antonio stood staring down at her. One hand propped on the windowsill above his head, the other on his hip. Reflected light from the morning sun glimmered over his handsome face like beams off icicles. He exuded power, a charismatic force that could reach across a flower garden and touch her like the caress of a hand.

Their eyes locked and Carina's breath caught in her throat. His expression was thoughtful; his brows drawn together as if something troubled him.

For a fleeting moment that seemed like aeons, she remained absolutely motionless. Then with a slight wave of his hand he withdrew from sight.

An electrifying shiver reverberated through her. She hugged her arms to herself.

Carina entered the kitchen determined to ignore this sudden, unwanted attraction she felt for Juan Antonio. Like a mantra, she cataloged all his faults in her mind, and boy did he ever come up lacking.

At the nonappearance of Alejandra, Carina had decided to prepare breakfast, and set about making tea while bacon sizzled in the pan. Never having acquired the taste for coffee, she knew she'd mess up if she tried to make it. To her way of thinking, a cold glass of iced tea would be much better with a bacon-and-egg *taquito.*

In the middle of rolling a tortilla stuffed with bacon

and egg, she jumped as an arm went around her waist and Juan Antonio's voice caressed her ear. "Mmm, I could get used to this." The underlying boldness of his suggestion captivated her. She remained silent.

"Ahhh," he exclaimed with a trace of laughter in his voice. "A woman after my own heart. Iced tea for breakfast."

"You like iced tea with breakfast?" She sidestepped him to get to the plates. "No kidding?"

"No kidding." He turned the glass up and she stared at the taut smoothness of his neck, the rest of his appearance slowly seeping beneath her defenses.

His shirt hung open, exposing a sleek, tan chest. Pants rolled into a cuff above his ankles, barefoot, with hair still ruffled by sleep.

Carina bit hard on her lower lip so no sound would burst out. *Lord, give me strength!*

Her green eyes met his black ones. He seemed very pleased with himself and she struggled to capture her composure.

"Breakfast is served." She placed the plate on the cabinet top in front of him and carried hers to the table.

"You only made one *taquito* for me?" He stared at his plate in disbelief.

"No, actually, I made two for me. Out of the kindness of my heart, I'm sharing one with you." Let him chew on that for a while. Carina boldly met his eyes as she sank her teeth into the first bite. He looked at her plate and moved to the table, the dark eyebrows arched mischievously.

"Then thanks very much for sharing, Miss Garza."

"My pleasure, Mr. Fuentes. Think you could reach behind you for my tea?"

"Sí, señorita." He set her tea beside her plate and ate his food with relish.

"Where is Alejandra? I searched the house for her but she's not here. And what are you doing sleeping so late? Yesterday, you were up with the chickens. And how did my luggage get here?" Glancing up at him, she frowned slightly.

"Ale has probably gone to the market. I left a note asking her not to wake us and not to bother with breakfast.

"Just so you know, originally, Alejandra came to help while the fruit inspector was in residence. When you left—" he winked at her as if he had nothing to do with her leaving "—there was no reason for her to stay. I attend to my own needs. So, I was going to send her back to her home."

"You mean this is not her home?" A tumble of confused thoughts and feelings assailed her.

"No, she lives with family in Tepic. Her salary for the next six months would have finished the apartment behind her son's home. She planned to move into it so the new daughter-in-law could have privacy."

"And now?" Carina questioned.

"Now?" he parroted.

"Are you going to let her stay?" Carina kept all expression from her voice when she asked. Her plans for the next six months hinged on his answer.

After several moments of silence, Carina glanced up at him. His eyes studied her with a curious intensity.

"Against my better judgment, I've already decided that she will stay."

Carina's heart sang in delight. Before she uttered a word of thanks, he held up a cautioning hand.

"Carina, listen very carefully. If you do not abide by my words, you may not stay here. There is too much danger in this job for you to go out alone. So, I'll take you to each site and work with you. You agree to this?"

Carina grabbed his hand in a tight grip. She felt elated. Nothing could please her more than to have him with her.

"I agree." She spoke with quiet but happy firmness.

"Somehow, that doesn't make me feel any better." Juan Antonio reclaimed his hand and with a piece of tortilla he scooped the remains of bacon and egg from the plate into his mouth.

Uncertain whether he teased or spoke the truth, she uncurled from her chair and carried her plate to the sink.

"Juan Antonio." She stared out the window above the sink and carefully spoke the next words. "I promise to abide by your rules as much as possible. I have no desire to prove anything to you or anyone else for that matter." Carina poured dishwashing soap into the running water. "I just want to do the job I was sent here to do."

She felt the brush of a hand on her back as he leaned around her to place his plate in the water.

"What made you choose agriculture as a profession in the first place?"

She raised her chin with a cool stare in his direction, but encountered a gleam of genuine interest in his eyes. He refilled his glass, then leaned back against the counter awaiting her reply.

Carina rinsed the soap from the dish in her hands.

"I love growing things. Since childhood, I've helped my parents plant vegetable and flower gardens. The entire process, from planting season to harvest, fascinates me."

She lifted the pan from the stove into the water.

"In Texas, in the Valley where I live, the entire year is a growing season of some type. My dad was a migrant worker and when the yield harvested, we would glean the fields. My brothers and I argued over who gathered the most onions or broccoli. We hated the cabbage because it..." Carina heard her voice, rising with excitement and abruptly stopped speaking.

"Yes?" There was a trace of laughter in his voice. "You hated the cabbage because?"

She glanced quickly at him for some sign of true emotion but he stared lazily back at her.

"Because it smelled so bad, like something soured." She chuckled in spite of herself. "Freddy said it smelled like a sickroom and amazingly he came down with something the very week we harvested. Year after year."

Carina wiped the table clear and then rinsed her dishcloth in the running water, swishing suds from the sink. Draping the cloth over the counter she dried her hands and looked around for lotion.

"Freddy is your brother, right?"

Carina nodded. "Yes, and I have another brother, Jesse. He is the oldest." She crossed to the table, curled one leg in under her and sat down.

"What do these brothers do? What are their jobs?" He chugged the rest of his iced tea and set his glass in the sink. He wiped his mouth with his hand, then rubbed his hand against his shirt, holding it for a second over his heart, patiently waiting for her answer. Carina swallowed hard.

How insane it was to be affected so by this man. This could not be happening to her. Scrambling for control, she rallied her thoughts.

"Jesse is a U.S. Border Patrol agent with ICE and Freddy is a professor at Pan Am University." She shrugged and said offhandedly, "I'm the only child that inherited both parents' green thumbs."

"And from whom did you inherit this tendency to land smack in the middle of disaster?" He leaned toward her, one eyebrow cocked questioningly, black eyes daring her to argue.

"Believe it or not, that happens only when I'm around…" Carina pointed at him "…you."

Quicker than lightning, his hand closed around her wrist and he drew her from the chair and into his arms. She flattened her palms against his chest.

Cupping her chin, he searched her upturned face.

"Scared this might turn into another disaster?" he questioned tentatively, as if testing the idea.

Surprised, Carina nodded. Taking a deep, unsteady breath she stepped back.

He touched his forehead in a mock salute then strode to the hallway, calling back over his shoulder, "Get ready and as soon as I'm dressed we'll go meet the masses."

She fell into a chair and rested her head on her hand. What was this obvious flirtation about? This was new to her but it felt good.

Chapter 6

Carina exclaimed in delight as the plane swept out over the Pacific Ocean low enough to capture smiles from fishermen casting their nets for shrimp.

"Oh, Juan Antonio, this is wonderful." Carina waved at the men, then tightly grasped the arms of her seat as Juan Antonio banked the plane at a forty-degree angle circling the boat, then slowed to land on the sandy beach.

Carina unclenched her fingers and relaxed her head against the seat.

"Whew!" She turned to look at Juan Antonio. "What a rush!"

"Yeah?" Juan Antonio pulled his headset off then reached to help her.

"Yeah." Carina leaned forward and paused while

he untangled her hair as he lifted her headset from her head. "Ouch."

"Sorry about that."

"So, you think all the plantation owners will be at this restaurant today?" She watched as he stowed the headsets away.

"They eat *desayuno* together every Wednesday morning. That's today. They'll be there." He pushed the door open, then held it with his foot. "Stay put and I'll come around and help you out."

"It's a little late in the day to be eating breakfast, don't you think?"

"No, I don't think. This is Mexico. The land of 'No one gets in a hurry,' remember? They'll be there, Carina. Have faith."

"Okay, okay. I guess I'm just a little nervous."

"Carina, for today, let me handle everything, *intende?* Then *mañana* I will work for you and you will be the *jefa* and boss me around. *Esta bien?*"

"*Sí,* Antonio, *esta bien.*" *That's fine with me, but I'll have to see it to believe it,* Carina reflected with a touch of bitterness.

Carina stepped out onto sand so white it made her squint even though she wore sunglasses. The Pacific Ocean crashed onto the beach on her left and coconut trees lined the shore on her right. Grass huts blended among the few cement houses, along with a small building bearing a sign reading *Miramar Hotel.*

A white golf cart pulled up alongside the plane, and as it slowed to a stop, a small child tumbled over the side and barreled straight at them. The sight reminded Carina of tumbleweed rolling end over end. "Tony, Tony, Tony" rang out joyously as the little feet touched the ground, identified the moving object as feminine, and Carina estimated her age at around three.

She watched in wonder as Juan Antonio caught the child up, swinging her round and round above his head till she screamed, then lowered her to receive a solid-sounding smack as the child kissed his cheek and little arms circled his neck.

"Tonio. *Como estas?*" A tall, white man approached, his voice heavy with an American accent. The same tight, blond curls covered his head as did the child's.

What is a gringo with a child doing way down here? Carina's thoughts were interrupted as Juan Antonio drew her forward with a touch to her shoulder, the other hand holding securely the arm of the child who now rode on his back.

"Carina, this is Rick Garrett. He and his wife are missionaries and live here on the island. Rick, Carina Garza is the Ag agent from the States."

"Nice to meet you, Carina. Welcome to Novillero." Carina caught the quick questioning glance he shot Juan Antonio before he shook her hand.

"And this—" Juan Antonio bent sideways and pulled the child around front "—is Abby, my favorite girl in the whole world."

"Pleased to meet you, Abby." Carina reached out to smooth the irresistible curls. The child stuck a finger in her mouth then hid her face against Juan Antonio. "Oh, she's shy."

"Yeah, right!"

"No es verdad." Juan Antonio and the child's father denied her assumption simultaneously then both laughed.

They piled in the golf cart, Juan Antonio placing

Abby beside Carina in the backseat. She tentatively drew the little girl close for safety's sake, prepared for a small amount of resistance, but Abby kept her head down and rested quietly in Carina's arms.

Rick stopped in front of the hotel, but the two men continued their conversation, neither showing any signs of leaving the golf cart. Carina sat waiting, happily observing the scene around her.

The hotel faced the beach and couldn't have boasted more than three rooms. Joining the side of the hotel, a thatched roof covered an area three times the size of the building. Smack in the middle, white plastic tables and chairs bearing the name of a popular beer encircled a round kitchen that looked similar to a gazebo. The only difference was the lack of lattice, and the windows that slid shut, completely enclosing the place.

Abby shifted from Carina's arms and leaned forward across the front seat, interrupting the men. "Daddy, I go see Mommy."

"In a moment, sweetheart."

Juan Antonio swung out of the cart, the happiness of moments before absent from his face. He stood beside Carina and extended his hand. "Ready?"

She placed her hand in his, preparing to step out when two little hands pressed against Carina's knees and a little body squeezed between her and the front seat, trying to exit first.

"I go, too, Tony."

"No, no, Abby. You stay with me," her dad said.

Expecting tears and arguments, Carina smiled in approval as Abby puckered up, then returned a finger to her mouth, remaining quiet.

Juan Antonio bent and kissed Abby's forehead.

"I'll see you in a little bit, baby girl. Okay?"

"Bye, Tony," she mumbled.

Juan Antonio strode purposefully around the back of the kitchen, still holding Carina's hand. Seated behind the kitchen, she counted nine men, laughing and talking, enjoying breakfast together. At the head of the table, Don Diego appeared to be in charge, describing in detail his plan to scare the *wetta* back to the United States. Carina couldn't help the shocked gasp that escaped and looked to see what Juan Antonio thought of this turn of events.

Juan Antonio waited, poised, like a mountain lion ready to pounce. When the laughter stopped suddenly, Don Diego turned to look behind him.

"Fuentes." Anger, swiftly masked, crossed Don Diego's features as he ground out Juan Antonio's last name. "I thought you'd be on your way to Tepic by now."

"Change of plans, Don Diego." Juan Antonio pulled Carina in front of him. "*Amigos.* Allow me to present Carina Garza, our new Ag agent." He acknowledged everyone, calling out each name as the two of them walked around the table and she shook hands. Only two of the men looked her in the eye.

"Now. Let me tell you how this thing is going to play out. Ms Garza and I will fly to Don Diego's tomorrow morning, where we will work the next couple of days. In the following weeks, she will inspect each of your orchards. If there are no problems—" Juan Antonio paused, one hand on the back of Don Diego's chair, the other on the table in front of him "—Ms. Garza's report to the States will be favorable. If Ms. Garza is met with resistance or all regulations are not in compliance with NAFTA's free trade laws—" Juan Antonio walked to the other end of the table facing Don Diego "—then *I* will make the report to the U.S. *Comprende?*" He finished speaking and stood, feet spread apart, arms folded across his chest. His eyes did not once move from the older man's face.

Carina stood frozen in place, waiting for Don Diego's response. Juan Antonio obviously had a reason for withholding the information from the others about the disease in the older man's orchard.

Don Diego laid his napkin beside his plate and stood.

"We will expect you and Señorita Garza in the morning, Señor Fuentes." He turned and walked away. A middle-aged man rose and followed close behind him.

Carina expelled her breath slowly, her mind struggling to comprehend all she'd just seen and heard. The men who were still seated spoke with Juan Antonio, but their expressions revealed their confusion as to what had just taken place.

"Ready?" While she'd been watching the men, Juan Antonio walked up beside her.

"Yes, I'm ready. I guess." Indecision ate at her. This was not the first impression she wanted to make on these men.

They walked from under the bamboo roof onto the highway. So far, this was the only paved road she'd seen and it ran right down the middle of the village. Several streets, made of round rocks from the ocean, exited off on each side. Carina absently watched a car approach them and its wheels bounced like a vehicle crossing a railroad track.

"You're awfully quiet. Should I be thankful?" He reached out and pulled her to the side of the road to permit a truck to pass them.

"Juan Antonio, why... What... Back there... I don't understand. And where are we going? Why are we walking in the heat of the day?"

"We're going to Rick and Marsha's. Another few yards and we'll be at their street. You don't mind, do you?"

"No, I don't mind." To the left of them, in front of a small mini super, stood six children in school uniforms. They looked to be about five years old and waited in line to buy a snack. The mini super's checkout desk covered the entire storefront, so customers were left no choice but to point to what they wanted or just hand the *señora* a list.

"Look, Antonio. Aren't they cute?" She pointed to the children straining to see over the countertop.

"Mmm," he responded vaguely.

They turned down the side street and Carina found it difficult to walk on the round stones, even though their surfaces were smooth. When she placed one foot on a stone and lifted the other foot to take a step, the foot on the rock would slip off, causing her to wobble. She glanced up to see how Juan Antonio managed. He walked calmly along the side of the street in the smooth path made by the villagers and many bicyclers.

"You heathen."

His burst of laughter drowned out her exclamation.

"You could have told me to walk over there."

"And miss the chicken dance exhibit? Not a chance."

"I guess I should pay attention to what's going on." She stepped onto the smooth path, her shoulder occasionally brushing his as they walked along.

"What's on your mind, Carina? Let's have it."

"Why would you think something's on my mind?"

"That little frown line on your forehead. You're quiet, distracted." He turned his head and their eyes met. "You know, pouting really doesn't suit you."

Carina stopped dead in her tracks.

"Pouting?" she screeched. "You think I'm pouting?" She struggled to lower her voice. "You, you, ah-hhhhh…" she sputtered. "I don't have time to pout. Thanks to you, I have this monstrosity of a mess hanging over my head. I have to…"

"What mess?" he interrupted. "I just straightened everything out for you, paved the way for you to continue working."

"No, you just 'paved the way' for *you*." She jabbed her finger at him. "Now I have to soothe everyone's egos so that they will work with me and not against me." Carina was so agitated she was practically in a jog. She slowed down.

Juan Antonio said, "I had nothing at stake in this. Well, at least not in this instance. I did this for you. To, to…" his shoulders lifted, his hand swept out in defense "…to right the injustice of Don Diego's actions last night. They got the message."

"They," she emphasized, "didn't need to get the message. Just Don Diego. Did you see the confusion on their faces? They had no idea what you were getting at. They were embarrassed for their *compadre*."

"They understood perfectly. Have you forgotten that Don Diego was entertaining the men with details of your fright as we approached their table?"

"But a few words spoken to Don Diego in private could have turned this whole thing around. He will not forget that you embarrassed him in front of his friends and he will oppose me at every turn. So will the others.

They will blame me, that an *amigo* suffered this—this," she stammered, "dishonor. Open rebuke."

"*Ay, caramba.* I cannot believe that you are so ungrateful."

"Ungrateful?" She felt her eyebrows rise to the tip of her bangs.

"Yes. Those men will respect you now. You will have no trouble from them. They have been warned. Only a woman would think like you do."

"Yeah?"

"*Exacto.*"

"Well, let me enlighten you as to why women think like that. One word: *experience.*"

What am I doing? Carina's thoughts interrupted her tirade with a bang. *This man also has the power to cost me this job.* Fury almost choked her. She couldn't afford to voice that anger so she fumed silently. How she would love to just once tell a man exactly what she thought of his attitude, but at whose expense in this case? Her own.

"Experience?"

"Never mind. I'm sorry I brought it up. Are we almost there? I sure could use some lemonade." She switched to damage control automatically, like a well-worn record.

"Carina…"

"Juan Antonio, let's enjoy this glorious day here and forget all previous events, okay? You're right. I'm being ungrateful. I'm sorry. Of course I appreciate all you've done for me."

She returned his gaze steadily, her mind resolved. She knew this routine well. Stroke the ego. Appear thankful to have a big, strong man making decisions for you. Her smile wavered not an inch.

* * *

Juan Antonio stared at the beauty looking solemnly back at him. He sensed strongly that he'd just been patronized. This sudden change of attitude sat at odds with her usual sassiness. Just seconds ago, she'd taken him to task for his actions; now she oozed compliancy.

"Juan Antonio. How nice to see you." He watched Carina's swift turn at Marsha's greeting, and grunted as Abby hurled herself against him.

"Marsha, hi. How are you?" He switched Abby over to his side. "This is Carina Garza, the new fruit inspector. Carina, Marsha Garrett. Wife to Rick, mother to Luke, Jonathan, Seth, Andy, Logan, Caleb and Abby."

"Wow!" Carina laughed as she shook the other woman's hand. "You have your hands full. Pleased to meet you."

"Likewise, and I can't begin to tell you how happy I am to have another female around. One of these days, Abby's going to be lots of company, but right now she's just one of the gang." Marsha's natural vivaciousness enveloped Carina, and Juan Antonio watched the passive expression fade from her features.

"So, you're gonna be nit-pickin' the fruit-pickin'."

Marsha led Carina into the house, their mingled laughter floating back to him. The conversation cut off when the door shut. Juan Antonio looked down at Abby, now scrambling to catch something in the grass.

"What are you up to, *mi hija?*"

"Wuana." She spoke through gritted teeth, both hands extended in a tight fisted grip.

"Easy, baby. Want me to take it?"

"Mmm-hmm." She released the baby iguana with a

little jump. "Let's show Mommy." She continued little jumps to the door.

"Mommy, Mommy, I ketched a wuana. Look Mommy, I ketched it." She whirled back to him reaching for the green lizard.

"Oh, Abby. You're worse than your brothers." Marsha ran a finger over the iguana's rough side. "Now put that back outside and don't torture him. Get washed up before your brothers get here."

Juan Antonio held the door open for Abby to pass. Laughter bubbled up in him and he glanced over to see Carina's response to the sight Abby made with her little arms held out, the iguana squeezed tightly. Their gazes met in shared amusement, then it seemed a shutter snapped and she turned and walked to where Marsha stood stirring something at the stove.

Well, so much for the sucking-up routine of moments before. Just like a woman to be so emotional. Happy one minute, sad the next, twisting a man's insides till he doesn't know how to act, believe or feel.

"Mom, we're home." Juan Antonio stepped aside, busy trading swats, high fives, down-lows and fist-bumps, as the gang of brothers entered, happy, hungry and loud.

"Boys, boys. Quiet down. We have company. This is Carina Garza. Come say hi." At their mother's coaching, each boy approached, shook Carina's hand, then returned to Juan Antonio's side.

"So, you finally have a girlfriend," Luke teased, his fifteen-year-old body tall and gangly. "Or do old men like you call them girlfriends?"

"Old? Who're you calling old?" Juan Antonio grabbed him around the neck, fake punching him in the side. "I can still whip your tail. And she's not my girlfriend. She's the new fruit inspector."

"Wash up, guys. Now!" Marsha commanded. "Oh, good. You're here." She smiled as Rick came in, pushing Abby along in front of him. "Now we can eat. Run and wash your hands, Abby."

Juan Antonio seated himself as Marsha and Carina began to set bowls of homemade soup at each place. Everyone scooted around the table, leaving an open place for Carina in the front. Abby crawled into the chair beside Juan Antonio. Marsha set a small plate of fish sticks in front of her.

"She won't eat soup," she explained, placing the catsup bottle near Abby.

"Let's pray." Rick said. "Jonathan?"

Jonathan nodded at his dad, muttered a few words and everyone dug in. Juan Antonio kept Carina under close observation during all of this, gauging her response to this wild bunch. Her glance whipped back and forth from one person to the next, she smiled steadily, but when their eyes chanced to meet, the smile slipped and her eyes lost their glow.

"Tonio, you'd better help her with that." Marsha nodded her head toward Abby. "Ahhh, too late."

Juan Antonio jerked backward, the blob of catsup sliding down the middle of his shirt. He grabbed the napkin and wiped, but the stain worsened.

He rounded the table intent on using a wet dishcloth.

"Here. This works better."

Shock held him in place as water soaked his shirt. Carina stood staring him down, the sprayer from the sink aimed at the stain on his shirt. She showed no sign of letting up and water began to cover the band of his pants. Aware of the thundering silence, he took the sprayer from her hand and returned it to the sink. He grasped her arm, turned to face his friends now shielding their eyes in embarrassment.

"Rick. Marsha. Thanks for your hospitality. Please excuse us."

Once outside, he dropped her arm like a hot potato. Anger simmered just beneath the surface. He walked beside her, all the way to the plane, never uttering one word. Why had he wanted to introduce her to his friends? He was just like his dad: he fell for the charm, the softness of a woman. Where did it get him? With his pride underneath her perfect little feet, that's where. Women! All they were good for was to chew you up, spit you out and leave you lying in a wasteland of want. Not anymore! He was through.

Chapter 7

Dear Lord. What have I done! Following behind Juan Antonio as he climbed into the plane, Carina stepped on the wing brace and pulled herself up to the door of the plane. That Juan Antonio silently fumed was evident in the absence of his help. She didn't blame him one bit. And the faces of those children… She was mortified.

"I…" She cleared her throat. She glanced at Juan Antonio's set face. He'd already put on his headset, and from the look of things was about to start the plane whether she was in or not.

"I have to go back." She turned, left the door hanging open and jumped off the step.

"Hey! Carina. Now what?" Juan Antonio's shout spurred her on. She ran down the side street they'd walked on their return to the plane. Or rather marched. Stomped?

Out of breath, she knocked on the Garretts' door and Rick stepped aside, allowing her to enter.

Carina glanced around the table, at the faces studying her solemnly. Marsha stood, took an uncertain step toward her, then stopped.

"Um, I want to apologize for my actions. I don't know what came over me, but I was wrong and rude to do something like that in your home in front of you and your precious children." She glanced first at Marsha then at Rick. "I'm so sorry," she said in a choked voice. "I'm just, um, totally baffled—" she raised her hand in appeal then dropped it to her side "—by my behavior."

"Oh, I think I might have some insight along those lines." Caught off guard at the humor in Marsha's voice, Carina merely stared wordlessly.

"Come with me." Marsha hooked her arm through Carina's and led her into the living room. "Do you know how long it's been since I've enjoyed a good 'girl talk' session?"

Carina gasped in delight as she entered the room.

"Oh, Marsha. This is lovely." Carina strolled about, touching a ceramic vase, then fingering a wool blanket hanging on the wall. Woven rugs boasting pyramid designs lay on a shiny terracotta tile floor. Pottery painted with cactus and donkeys lined the stair wall. A saddle and sombrero hung on a rack that looked like a quilting frame. "Your kitchen is so modern, so American. I'd never have dreamed this part would be so authentic. It's beautiful."

"Thank you. This was Rick's baby. I did the kitchen and our bedroom, he did the living room and study. The kids all had a hand in decorating their rooms, so we have a smattering of the two cultures all through the house."

"Well, it works. You're very talented and so special to be missionaries in a land foreign to all you've ever known." At Marsha's nod toward the sofa, Carina sank into the soft leather that cradled her in comfort. "And I am so embarrassed by my actions in front of your family." She closed her eyes, reliving the scene and groaned. "How could I have done something so stupid? Did you see his face?" She pressed a hand over her mouth to stem the hysterical laughter threatening to escape.

"Oh, yes." Marsha giggled. "That was priceless." She mimicked Juan Antonio's shocked and then stoic expressions and dissolved into gales of delight.

Carina clutched one of the throw pillows to her chest then buried her face in it, allowing laughter to relieve the tension that wound her tight. She laughed till tears ran down her face and even more when Marsha couldn't seem to gain control and smacked the arm of the chair she sat in.

"Oh, law. We've got to stop this. Rick's gonna come in here and think we've lost our marbles." Marsha wiped her eyes. "Then he'll want to pray for us." That set them both off again until finally Carina laid her head back against the sofa, once again astonished at the ever-changing mystery of emotions.

"Marsha, why on earth would I act like that? I haven't a clue as to what came over me. Actually, I am mortified. I've never done anything like that in my whole life."

"Maybe you're more attracted to Juan Antonio than you're letting on or admitting to yourself."

"What do you mean?"

'Well, before Rick and I became an item, we dated a couple of times and I almost instantly fell in love. His actions toward me said he felt the same, but he never spoke the words. One day he asked me to go to a mission board meeting with him. They began to ask questions, then we were separated and questioned in private. I thought Rick was using me to gain a position with this board. I mean, why else would he bring me here? He'd mentioned no plans for the future with me. Spoken no words of love. Nothing.

"So, when the president asked me how I felt about expository preaching, you know th—"

"Yes, I know," Carina interrupted. "Verse-by-verse explanation of the scriptures."

"Yeah, well, I told them I didn't like it. I said that a pastor or preacher should just read a verse or two and get up and say what God placed on his heart. That expository preaching was overrated and boring."

A shocked gasp escaped Carina. "Oh, no! What happened?"

"They brought us back in front of the panel of men and informed us that we weren't accepted because of differences in our beliefs. They quoted that scripture about how can two walk together except they be agreed."

"And?"

"Rick questioned them about the differences and they explained that a missionary's main form of spreading the gospel was through expository preaching. He quickly assured them he believed the same thing. They replied, 'Come back once you've convinced your wife.'"

"Yikes."

"Oh, yeah."

"So what happened next?"

"Rick just sat there, then he turned to look at me. I will never forget that look as long as I live. He acted almost precisely like Tonio. He stood, thanked the board for their time, took my arm in a viselike grip and marched us out of there."

"He apparently forgave you. You're still together."

"Once we ironed out all the difficulties, things sailed smoothly along. So you see? This could be the exact reason you did what you did."

"Huh?" Carina shook her head in confusion. "You've lost me."

"Well, maybe you acted out of frustration. Could be you're developing feelings for Tonio and are upset that he hasn't revealed his feelings for you. In other words, you don't know where you stand."

"Oh, no, no, no. You have it all wrong. So far, I've spent more time angry at him or disappointed. We've only had a moment or two where we actually…" She stammered to a halt. "Argh, he makes me so frustrated."

"He's very good-looking," Marsha said with a trace of humor in her voice.

"Looks don't matter when you argue each point. Or at least I feel like I'm going to have to argue my point."

"He's so intelligent."

Carina sprang from the sofa. "Oh, yeah! He's intelligent."

"And he's really good with kids."

"Marsha." Carina stopped pacing, and with hands on hips regarded her new friend in mock anger. "Whose side are you on, anyway?"

Marsha stood and pulled Carina into a quick embrace. "I'm on both sides. I hope something comes of this. Tonio's fought his own private problems for some time and I'd love to see him head over heels in love. You know, the kind that pushes logic right out the window. By the way, one of these days you'll look back on today and laugh."

They strolled back into the kitchen chuckling together and Carina looked straight into serious black eyes that regarded her steadily. "Oh, I don't know about that," she said. "I just don't think so."

Chapter 8

"Ready?" Tired, hungry and dirty, Juan Antonio wanted nothing more than to be at home, reclined back in the chair on the front porch looking out over the ocean. What a week it had been.

"Yes, I'm ready. Just let me give this sample to Pancho."

Juan Antonio watched Carina's weary walk to Don Diego's sapling shed. Her shoulders drooped and her footsteps dragged.

For weeks now, they'd worked from five-thirty in the morning until seven-thirty at night. Each day, respect grew for Carina. Her stamina, intelligence and patience were astounding and she kept all samples in meticulous order. By the end of the first day, she'd won over Pancho, and *poco y poco,* Don Diego's attitude softened toward her.

It became increasingly clear that she intended to salvage what she could of his produce. She'd ordered a fungicidal treatment from Mexico City, but they couldn't deliver for fourteen days, so she had barrels flown in overnight at NAFTA's expense.

Juan Antonio followed her from field to field, observing, listening and learning. If any of the workers offered suggestions, she considered them and oftentimes opted for their ideas. If suggestions went contrary to the benefit of the orchard, she patiently explained, courteously asking if they understood.

The first day, due to the lateness of the hour, Don Diego offered them rooms in his hacienda, and they accepted. Early next morning Juan Antonio flew home for clothes and toiletries, and to talk to his own manager. Today they'd worked half a day but finally were going home for much-needed rest; their first time alone together since the shambles of that Wednesday with the Garretts.

She and Marsha had entered the kitchen arm in arm, smiling. She looked him straight in the eyes then her glance shied away. Still, she walked bravely to where he sat, and apologized. Her voice, low and husky, had awakened feelings so strong he had to fight the urge to crush her to him and explore the powerful emotions she stirred.

Then sanity returned and so did his thought processes. Bit by bit she slipped beneath his self-erected barriers, though he fought hard not to allow it. She was a woman and that was their trademark. They sank their tentacles deep, until a man lost all reasoning, till he caved in and became weak. Like his dad.

So, he had bowed toward her slightly and said, "Apology accepted," and they spent the rest of the day playing with the kids and grilling fajitas, returning home with a temporary truce between them.

She walked toward him now, fatigue settled in pockets under her eyes. She rubbed a spot on her face and left a smudge of dirt behind. He gently removed the spot with his thumb. The heavy lashes that shadowed her cheeks flew up and she stared, wordlessly. And when she looked at him like that, a spark of power lit up inside his soul.

His chest felt as if it would burst but he managed to say calmly, "Let's go home." He took her hand, walked to the Suburban, drove to the airstrip and flew to the hacienda, and remembered nothing of the trip. Fear tore at his insides. He was fighting a losing battle to keep her at arm's length.

Carina stood beneath the shower, the tepid water not quite adequate for washing away her fatigue. She'd lived on adrenaline for weeks now and felt totally exhausted and on edge. The exhaustion would be nonexistent by the end of the day; it was the other that had her emotions erratic and turbulent.

She felt like a breathless girl of eighteen with each glance Juan Antonio cast her way, and when he touched her she felt wrapped in invisible warmth.

That's how lust usually makes one feel, dodo brain. But it doesn't have anything to do with love, not one iota. She wrapped a towel around her head and slipped into a white terry cloth robe. *Look how many men the heroine went through in* Runaway Bride, *before she ever found Mr. Right, and she certainly felt something for each one. And you're gonna have to do just like she did if you fall for this man. You'll have to alter your life-style to suit his. If his preference is* huevos ranchero, *you'll have to like eggs and salsa. If it's* huevos cocidos, *boiled eggs it will be.*

She climbed on the bed, hooked her chin over her knee and swept the first coat of iced champagne nail polish over her toenails.

Well, I just won't eat any more eggs. Problem solved.

And what will you do when he dictates where you go, who you're with, what you wear...?

All right, already. I get the point.

Relaxing back on her elbows, she scissored her legs back and forth to dry the nail polish.

He's so handsome.

Oh, puh-lease! Give me a break. Twenty years down the road, and five kids later, how good's he gonna look?

Well, since he won't be the one having the kids, I'd say he'll probably look hot, and I'll look like Mount St. Helens.

Hummph. Since you won't be serious, I'm through trying to talk sense into you.

Good. Let's get dressed and go bask in Tonio's un-deniable magnetism.

Yes, let's.

Huh? I thought you were the voice of reason in my head.

Well, you know what they say. If you can't lick 'em, join 'em. Now, what are we gonna wear?

Carina, you are totally and completely certifiably insane.

Acutely aware that fatigue prevented her from ana-lyzing the disquieting thoughts that troubled her lev-elheaded mind, Carina inclined her head in a small gesture of defeat. In truth, she didn't want to fight this magnetic pull between them, but gut instinct told her she should run for her life.

She heard the Suburban crank up and she jumped off the bed and ran to the window, watching the big vehicle leave the drive headed for the runway. She hadn't heard a plane buzz the house so she wondered where Juan Antonio was going.

She hurried downstairs. The table in the dining room was set for three and Carina was glad Alejandra would be joining them. Despite her short bout of insanity while dressing, she felt she needed a buffer between herself and Juan Antonio. So much had happened in the short time she'd been here and there had been no time to evaluate every little thing. Juan Antonio was an intense person, and when he switched all that intensity to her, unusual feelings crept up from somewhere near her heart.

As she worked with Don Diego's men, he'd stood in the background, vaguely disturbing in his role as protector and mediator. He had not interfered once in her decisions, but managed to stay one step ahead of her, anticipating her needs, which he'd quietly and discretely carried out without the first request from her to do so.

He had lightened her load considerably and, unbeknownst to him, he'd shared a whole scope of emotions with her. If she worked late into the night, her body tired and sore, his eyes brimmed with tenderness and compassion. When her actions seemed to amuse him, he teased and bantered, his mouth quirked with humor.

Once, when standard testing couldn't ascertain if a particular batch of mangos were ripe, she bit into one and the juice ran off her chin. She brought her hand up, trying to suppress her giggles. His eyes narrowed on her mouth and with his thumb he'd wiped her chin, his touch soft and caressing. Her heart hammered against her ribs and she leaned toward him, yearning for the kiss she knew would come next, but Don Diego stepped into the harvesting shed, ruining the moment.

Carina heard the Suburban return and went to greet Juan Antonio, her whole being filled with expectancy, an unexplainable excitement. His actions spoke of affection, kindness and attraction. They could build on that; perhaps Juan Antonio would be the great love of her life. She pulled the door open, allowing the joy his presence gave her to show on her features. She was not disappointed. His gaze riveted on her face. Something intense flared between them. With long purposeful strides he started toward her.

"Tony," an ultra-feminine voice wheedled. "Aren't you going to help me, baby?"

Carina merely stared, tongue-tied. Beautiful and stunning only partially described the girl standing beside the vehicle. With her lips pouting and her body stance a come-and-get-me pose, she looked as if she'd stepped right off the cover of a Hollywood magazine. Not much was left to the imagination. Acid burned in Carina's stomach, yet she hadn't eaten a bite of food.

Antonio stopped mid-stride and turned. "Sorry, munchkin." He followed her to the back of the SUV and removed several suitcases.

So we have company. Carina held the door as the two entered the hacienda. Antonio set the luggage at the foot of the stairs and before he could straighten to full height, the girl wrapped herself around his arm. "Oh, Tony, this is going to be so much fun. Just like old times." She swatted his arm then turned to acknowledge Carina.

"And who do we have here?"

"Munchkin, this is Carina Garza, the fruit inspector sent by NAFTA. Carina, this is April Garrett, Rick's baby sister."

Carina felt her eyes widen in surprise. This was Rick's sister? Tiny scraps of cloth covered strategic parts of the woman's body, but the majority of her beautiful exposed skin gleamed with silken smoothness.

"Oooh, yikes. You work in the fields? How horrible for you."

"Now, munchkin, how would you know that since you've never been to the fields, much less worked in one?" Juan Antonio answered before Carina recovered sufficiently from the other woman's rudeness.

"Exactly! And I never will work in one. Who would even want a job like that?"

"You know? Last time I looked I'm still here in the room." Exasperated at the obvious lack of manners, Carina launched a little dig of her own. "And where, pray tell, did you get the nickname 'munchkin'?" The woman stood six feet tall at least, and most of that height was leg; beautiful, tan, oiled legs.

Juan Antonio grabbed an arm of each woman and guided them toward the dining room.

"Ladies, ladies, let's not…ummm…"

"Squabble," Carina said, sarcasm dripping from her voice.

"Bicker," the "munchkin" said at the same time.

"Yes, yes, that's it." Juan Antonio accepted both interpretations, gently pushing them toward his destination.

As Juan Antonio politely seated the other woman, Carina pulled the chair out and seated herself. She would much rather have been at the smaller table in the kitchen where she and Juan Antonio had shared their first breakfast together. But this meal should prove entertaining to say the least. She glanced up and caught the other woman's assessing look. Surprisingly, there seemed to be a bit of insecurity, of vulnerability in the sudden downward swoop of her eyelids. Then with a forced vivaciousness she switched all attention to Juan Antonio and Carina sat back to enjoy the show.

"Remember, Tony, when we flew to Llano Grande and landed on the dirt runway on top of the mountain? Can we do that this trip?"

A war of emotions raged through Carina as she watched the woman caress Juan Antonio's arm, her bright red fingernails long enough to do major damage should she decide to strike.

"April, you screamed and cried and we had to force you back into the plane when it was time to return home. Why would we put ourselves through that again?" Juan Antonio's voice was laced with humor and Carina grudgingly admired the way he slipped his arm from the vixen's grasp.

April. So that was her name. Somehow it had slipped Carina's memory since the introduction. She would never be able to call the girl munchkin. She felt the corners of her mouth slip up. A munchkin April Garrett was *not!*

"Care to share with us? Carina?"

Juan Antonio's words finally registered on her dizzied senses.

"Share what?"

"Whatever it was that brought that beautiful smile to your face."

Mixed feelings surged through her. Was he purposely flirting with her in front of his guest? Did he want the other woman to see that there was something special happening between them? Was there something special? She stared, glimpsing a spark of some indefinable emotion in his expression. He prolonged the moment, not moving, not even a blink, till Carina felt a flush begin to climb into her cheeks. A satisfied light came into his eyes and he raised an eyebrow enquiringly. "The smile?"

"Oh. That." Carina sought a plausible explanation. She couldn't very well say she thought his nickname hilarious for the tall woman. "Just thinking private thoughts, I guess. Ah, here's Alejandra with our meal."

Carina reached to take the bowl of refried beans, her stomach growling. Rice and *pico de gallo* followed and then Alejandra carried in a steaming pan of fajitas covered in white cheese. Carina could hardly wait and bowed her head for prayer before the tortillas were set on the table. She silently asked the blessing and then raised her head to find Juan Antonio and April staring at her.

Juan Antonio's arm lay on the table, hand extended upward, waiting for her. She saw at a glance that he already held April's hand.

"I think we should pray together, Carina. How about it?" His left eyebrow rose and Carina slipped her hand in his, her lips parted in surprise. She'd eaten with him every day and not once had he prayed over his meal. He squeezed her hand and she realized she was still staring and the other two had closed their eyes. She hurriedly bowed her head and listened as he spoke, almost verbatim, the words she always said silently.

When he finished she stole a quick glance at him, her feelings becoming more and more intense. The look in his eyes was gentle and contemplative, as if he, too, sensed an intensified change happening between them.

"Oh, this smells so good. Thanks, Alejandra." April's voice snapped her from serious contemplation about a possible nonexistent relationship.

Surprised, Carina watched Alejandra place both hands on April's shoulders and April reach up and touch one of those hands. Apparently Alejandra liked the girl very much if her actions were any indication. However, Carina's annoyance increased when she caught the smirk on the other girl's face.

"So, Carmen, where do you hail from?"

"The name is Carina, and I was born and raised in Texas." She might as well establish her citizenship, though it probably wouldn't stop the girl from treating her like a "Mexican."

A warning flickered in her heart and she knew she had been unpleasing to the Lord in her unchristian thoughts about the other girl. Regret stirred uneasily and she hastened to make things right, whispering a silent plea for forgiveness from the Lord.

"And you, April? Where do you live?" Carina struggled for a friendlier tone of voice.

"I live in North Carolina." April's tone was dismissive and Carina recited a verse in her mind: *Blessed are the meek for they shall inherit the earth. Blessed are the meek...* Well, she'd inherited the earth, all right—at least the section with Don Diego's harvest. She'd do well to focus on her job and leave *munchkin* to Juan Antonio.

"Tony, let's you and I go on down to Novillero and spend the night at Rick and Marsha's. We can eat at the Miramar, then walk along the beach. Oh, that would be so much fun." April tilted her head and fit the last of a fajita in her mouth, chewed a few times then continued, allowing an irritating whine to enter her voice. "Please, Tony? I only have a couple of weeks here and I'd like to enjoy my time as much as I can."

Carina looked up to gauge Juan Antonio's reaction to the wheedling and was caught off guard to find him watching her. She stared wordlessly back, her heart pounding. "Yes, *Tony*—" she injected as much sarcasm as possible into her shaking voice "—why don't you show *munchkin* a good time while she's here?" Her thin fingers tensed in her lap. She hoped her smile was noncommittal. She would not, could not, play second fiddle to his attentions to another woman. Too many women of her race already did this for the male Don Juans and Romeos.

"I'm sorry, April." His heavy emphasis on the name and a direct look at Carina acknowledged her overuse of "munchkin." "We'll leave in the morning as planned. Carina and I worked half the day and I for one am tired and would like to rest."

They finished the meal in an awkward silence and when Juan Antonio suggested they retire to the front veranda, Carina excused herself and went to her room. She walked the length of her room with her phone held out, searching for a signal, finally finding one while standing in the shower stall. She placed a call to her mother updating her about the job and the success she'd had with Don Diego's produce. Her mother talked about Carina's brother, Jesse's promotion and what was currently blossoming in her garden. When Carina hung up it was still too early for bed, so she caught up on paperwork.

Out of the corner of her eye she saw a book that had tried to get her attention even before she'd called her mother. Now it called to her again and she knew there must be a special message waiting for her. She picked her Bible up and sat cross-legged on the bed. Her Bible fell open to Philippians 3:7. *But what things were gain to me, those I counted loss for Christ.*

She rubbed her finger over the underlined verse. What was the Lord saying to her?

Lord, I know what this scripture refers to and what Apostle Paul sacrificed for Christ, but all evening You've impressed me to read Your Word. So what exactly is this verse supposed to mean to me? She read it again and then backed up and read the entire chapter. Other words jumped out at her. *I count all things but loss for the Excellency of the knowledge of Christ Jesus and have no confidence in the flesh.*

She ran a couple of reference verses and enjoyed time spent with the Lord. Yet when she laid her head on the pillow, she still had no clue why the Lord touched her heart with those particular scriptures.

Chapter 9

Juan Antonio arose after a good night's sleep, shaved, showered, dressed and hurried to the study. He filed a flight report with the Mexican Aviation Association and then responded to an email from the real estate office in Mazatlan. He had planned to stay in Novillero till Carina finished work at the Rodriquez orchard, but the agent wanted to show the plantation to a potential buyer, so he confirmed his presence for the following Monday. He closed the email program and walked out onto the veranda. A cool breeze lifted the hair off his brow and added to his sense of well-being.

He stared out over mango trees as far as his eyes could see. His great-grandfather Oscar Fuentes had started the orchard with twenty trees and ten acres of land. His grandfather Oscar Antonio Fuentes had increased it by one hundred acres and three hundred trees.

Papi, his dad, had maintained the orchard as best he could, but the ravages of time had made their mark on the trees. His father had passed away a little over a year ago and Juan Antonio had taken over the mantle as a mango farmer.

His heart warred daily with his mind over the sale of something so precious to his forefathers. But he had no desire to live in Mexico. Although its people, for the most part, were generous, kind and hardworking, it was the other side of Mexico's culture he wished to avoid. The drug lords better known as the Zetas, or cartel, warred against the government and law officials. Law officials were corrupt and played both sides. Extortionists randomly robbed the rich, demanding exorbitant amounts of cash and most often receiving it, the alternative being a swift and certain death. His father's homeland had turned ugly and dangerous, and he was determined not to live his life in fear. Having been born in the United States, with his mother being an American citizen, and his father a Mexican national, he had dual citizenship. That worked well in his present circumstances. Only a Mexican citizen could sell land along the *frontera* or along the beach. He'd had no problems getting the deed and registering the land with an agent.

The client wanting to view the property had toured the plantation previously. According to the real estate agent, he planned to bring his family and his attorney. The agent also provided financial information on the man and Juan Antonio's price was no obstacle.

Juan Antonio rubbed his hands together in anticipation. His ranch in Texas would soon be attainable. When his dad died, his mother had divided equally between Juan Antonio and his two brothers the land she and his father co-owned in the United States. Five thousand acres of prime ranch land. Marcelo, the oldest, had a successful cattle ranch on the right side of the acres. Raul, the youngest, had chosen the home place and six hundred acres of Ruby Red grapefruits. Juan Antonio's part lay in the eastern section near the coast, and he planned to raise sugarcane.

He heard the click of high heels on the tile floor outside his office and knew April would soon enter his office. Carina would have better sense than to wear such outlandish shoes in the sand, the dirt and on cobblestone streets. How he knew this about her he wasn't sure. He just knew. He moved through the open French doors and stepped out of sight, hiding behind the front balustrade. He hoped to avoid more alone time with April. Carina had retired early the night before and he'd been forced to entertain the visitor. April had, however, proved to be a good conversationalist when she wasn't being a brat.

Twenty-six suddenly felt old. Not too very long ago, April would have been the kind of woman he'd have wanted by his side; someone who didn't require much of him besides money and position in life. Now he knew that would never satisfy. A relationship built on surface fluff would deteriorate over time, leaving him with a broken home—something he definitely didn't believe in. But then his parents were married thirty-four years before his dad died and Juan Antonio considered their marriage broken.

"Penny for your thoughts?"

He turned as soon as he heard Carina's voice.

"Not even worth a penny." He glanced at her shoes and grinned. "Leather-soled sandals."

She held her foot out for inspection. "Did I do something wrong?"

"You snuck up on me. I heard April coming a mile away."

He liked the way she looked him straight in the eye. "I knew it was her by the clacking of her heels." He met her one raised eyebrow of silent inquiry with a nod. "I hid."

"I'm sorry for intruding. I didn't realize you wanted to be alone." She turned to leave, but he reached for her hand, pulling her to his hiding place.

"I don't want to be alone. I like being with you." He felt a whole host of things as he looked into her eyes. Neither one of them seemed to have words to fit the moment. He waited several long minutes before he lowered his head.

Her mouth lifted in mute invitation, beautiful green eyes tempting with eager promises. Lips, soft and moist, brushed against his as she spoke. "I feel the same."

He knew the exact moment his heart became one with hers.

Carina shared a songbook with Juan Antonio but she sang alone, her alto voice blending with April's. A delightful sense of belonging filled her at how Juan Antonio placed her beside him in the plane, then again held her back as he motioned April into the pew first. April remained quiet through the plane ride, and only the toss of hair over her shoulder as she sat on the bench showed her agitation. Surrounded now by her niece and nephews, she seemed to accept the idea that a relationship between herself and Juan Antonio would not happen. She had her arm around one of the kids and she sang soprano beautifully on key; her pronunciation of the Spanish words *Hay poder en Jesus* clear, exact and phonetically correct.

Carina focused on the message Pastor Garrett delivered and tried hard to stifle a giggle when he accidentally said "five smooth dogs" instead of "five smooth stones." She pictured little David picking up five smooth puppies and throwing them at the giant Goliath. She glanced at Juan Antonio with his arms crossed on his chest and saw the corners of his mouth tip up. He turned his gaze on her, his eyes flashing a similar display of mirth.

Carina felt a warm glow flow through her and she tried hard to focus once more on the sermon. Just like Biblical David, she'd had some giants in her life, but they paled in comparison to this new experience; this exciting intimacy with another person.

April heaved a long sigh that caught Carina's attention. The girl was melting in front of them. Sweat trickled down the side of her face and she fanned vigorously with a songbook. Carina knew she'd be in the same predicament had she not been working out in the fields in the heat. Having acclimated to the weather she rather enjoyed the warm breeze wafting through the open windows.

There were so many differences in culture here in Mexico. Back home in Texas, not many churches would even have services if the air conditioning broke down. This church had no air conditioning; it didn't even have glass in the metal window frames. That's what Carina loved about old Mexico. People survived here without all the modern conveniences she'd grown accustomed to. Each day she met new challenges that tested her ability; her stamina. Several times while showering and before she could rinse shampoo from her hair the water had cut off. After the second time, she'd placed a bucket of water with a pitcher in the shower with her.

Almost every morning at ten, the electricity would go off and remain off till after lunch, which meant no fans or lights to work with. She'd moved most of her inspection tables outside in the natural light. None of these obstacles had been insurmountable, but the first couple of days had driven her crazy.

Now she took the difficulties in stride but had compassion for April, who had rubbed all the makeup off her face wiping away the sweat, and whose hair was plastered to her head. With a songbook Carina pretended to fan herself, knowing the extra air movement would help April. Her newly awakened sense of confidence in what was blossoming between herself and Juan Antonio placed her beyond intimidation. She felt powerful. Everything took on a clean brightness.

When the service ended, they walked the short distance from the church to the Garretts' house. Juan Antonio made funny faces at Abby as her small hands pressed against his cheeks. He carried her with ease and the patience he showed was admirable.

Several times, April's spiked heels stuck in the sandy earth and one of her nephews rescued her, mocking her choice of footwear. She didn't seem to mind and the camaraderie between them and their aunt revealed a tight bond of love and caring.

"I'm so glad you guys came this morning." Marsha tied an apron around her waist and washed her hands in the kitchen sink. "Kids, change your clothes. Abby,

I laid yours on the bed. Bring them to *Tia* April and she'll help you change."

"Come on, Skeeter. Let's go find your clothes." April swung the girl into her arms, growling kisses into her neck, making the little girl scream with delight. It was hard to associate the sexy vixen of yesterday with the loving aunt of today.

They feasted on *carne guisada, papas* and *ensalada.* Once again Juan Antonio maneuvered Carina into a chair next to his; an act that was evidently not lost on the observant Marsha. Carina could barely follow the conversation, seeing as there were six or seven going at the same time, but she enjoyed the storytelling and teasing and April was the center of attention. The change in her attitude amazed Carina and she found herself liking the girl despite her first impressions.

They sat around the table long after everyone finished and the smaller ones went down for naps. Juan Antonio had his hand wrapped around the chair post of Luke's chair, talking in a low voice to the boy about airplanes. From what Carina heard of the conversation, the Garretts' oldest son longed to be a pilot. Juan Antonio patiently answered his questions and encouraged him to study; not once did a discouraging word pass his lips, and admiration grew within Carina's heart.

"Carina, do you and Tonio plan to stay the week here with us?" Marsha's voice broke into her thoughts and Carina relaxed back against her seat, hands rubbing the bottom edge of the tablecloth that touched her lap.

"Yes, we brought our things with us. Are you sure it's not an imposition? We can stay at the Rodriquez place. It's no bother."

"No, no. I want you both here with me, and I'll admit

for selfish reasons." Marsha's laugh was infectious and
Carina knew why the Mexican people had accepted this
gringo couple into their lives. They cared. They truly
cared and it showed. "We start VBS in two weeks and
due to procrastination, I only have next week to dec-
orate and put together crafts and a menu. That's why
April's here. She comes every year and helps me get
things prepared and then she teaches a class."

"April teaches?" Carina could hear the disbelief in
her voice. She turned to look questioningly at the other
woman and barely controlled a gasp of surprise. April's
face reddened and she hung her head. Whether in embarrassment or false shyness, Carina didn't know nor
care. She did not judge people's actions but the party
girl from last night conflicted majorly with Vacation
Bible School teacher. Carina could only assume from
the girl's discomfort that she normally did *not* act that
way. She hastened to put April at ease.

"Where did you learn Spanish, April?"

"I grew up here in Novillero. Our parents are missionaries." At Carina's raised eyebrows and open-
mouthed surprise, April smiled and continued. "My
dad had some health problems and Rick and Marsha
took over the ministry."

"How wonderful." Carina rushed to clarify her statement. "Not that your dad had problems, but that you
grew up here and learned Spanish fluently. And the
ministry didn't stop."

Carina had never actually met a missionary in the
field before meeting Rick and Marsha, and this family really challenged her thoughts on the subject. She
always enjoyed the missionaries who passed through
their church services from time to time, especially the

ones with PowerPoint presentations, but as soon as they left she forgot about them. Now here was a family that knew no other lifestyle but that of serving God full-time. They were so friendly and by far the happiest people she'd ever met.

"Dad and Mom will be here the week of VBS," Rick added. "You'll get to meet them."

"Great."

He placed his arm around Marsha's shoulders, drawing her close for a kiss to her forehead. She propped against his side, very much at ease with his actions, and Carina knew a strong bond held together these two people raising a family in a foreign land. The Mexicans were her people but Carina was not sure she could give up the comforts of home in the United States to live in her dad's homeland. She twisted in her seat, uncomfortable with the directions her thoughts had taken.

Juan Antonio turned slightly toward her, stretching his arm across the back of her seat. His hand touched her hair as if to calm her, lingered a moment before he grasped the opposite-side chair post. "Let me just warn you right now, Carina—" his voice took on a menacing tone "—I am the favorite." Loud laughter erupted but he spoke loudly over the noise. "So don't go trying to win brownie points with the Garretts."

Everyone spoke at once and Carina didn't understand, until Marsha finally explained. "Mom and Dad Garrett think Tonio hung the moon. He flies them around in his plane, gives them all the mangoes they can eat, preserve and make jelly with. And if Mom starts to lift the slightest thing, Tonio rushes to the rescue. Just like when Dad had his heart attack. Tonio flew him to the hospital in Mazatlan and that's probably what saved his life."

Amid the good-natured teasing that followed, Carina studied Juan Antonio's profile. He looked uncomfortable with the compliment Marsha had paid him, but an expression of satisfaction showed in his eyes. He loved this family. Unbidden her mind went back to the day he'd flown her back to Tepic, ordering her to go home. Even then, he hadn't been mean-spirited to her, following her to the taxi stand trying to explain his decision. He turned to look at her, black eyes shining, and the connection was powerful. She felt as if she'd stepped into a wonderful world where God directed her present and future.

In a teasing voice she questioned, "What? A big man like you afraid of a little competition? Can I help it if I'm better at some things than you?" She watched his eyes widen and knew the challenge had been understood and accepted.

"Ah, man. That bites. You gonna let that pass?" Luke's protest rang with indignation.

"I think Carina's begging for a round of tag football."

Before Juan Antonio could rise from his seat and amid excited calls of agreement from the younger boys, Marsha intervened.

"It's three-fifty, guys, and we have to be back at church at six. We don't have time for a game, then showers for everyone." She pushed to her feet and placed a few glasses in the sink. "Besides, I want the girls to cut out crafts for the teens. So find something quiet to do because if you wake up Abby, you *will* tend to her." She wiped the table off while shooing the men off to the *sala*.

Juan Antonio gently pushed Carina along in front of him till they were out from behind the table, and with hands on her shoulders propelled her toward the living room with the men. She laughingly protested, trying to duck behind him, but he was stronger and faster than her.

"Tonio, I need to help Marsha."

He pulled her down beside him on the sofa and, truth be told, she had no desire to move. April, Luke and Jonathan piled around the coffee table and began a game of Phase Ten. So much for cutting out crafts with Marsha. When Rick saw the others occupied he whispered in Marsha's ear and she followed him to the bedroom. Carina noticed they left the bedroom door slightly ajar and wondered if they felt the need to chaperone.

Juan Antonio kicked back the recliner part of the sofa, stretched out his long sturdy legs and laid his head against the cushions, eyes closed. One arm lay along Carina's shoulder, the other across his eyes. The seat was big and easily accommodated them both, but Carina felt embarrassed and tried to shift onto the adjoining cushion. His arm tightened, holding her in place, loosening only when he felt her relax. She turned her back to him; a part of her reveled in his open display of affection, but her emotions soared off the charts at each touch, look or kind word from him. What had happened to the levelheaded young woman she prided herself on being? Her hands unconsciously twisted together.

He heaved an exaggerated sigh and then his arm, strong and massive, turned her to face him.

"You're killing me here." He spoke in a low, gentle tone, a faint light twinkling in his black eyes. "Stop thinking. Relax. Nothing will happen that you don't want."

Carina glanced quickly at the room's other occupants. They were engrossed in their games so she decided to satisfy a bit of curiosity.

"And if I like what's happening?" She stared into eyes that were gentle and contemplative.

"Have you ever had a boyfriend?"

"No." Distracted by the huskiness in his voice, Carina plunged on carelessly. "I mean, yes. I dated someone in college for three months but he said I was too bossy and that he already had a mother."

She felt the chuckle deep in his chest but all he said was *"Idiota."*

"And you?" An unwelcome blush crept into her cheeks. "Have you ever had a girlfriend?"

For a long moment he looked at her, reaching into her thoughts. One corner of his mouth twisted upward. "A few, but none of them serious."

"And what's happening between us? Is it serious?"

His expression stilled. His hand closed over hers, effectively halting her fingers' frenzied twisting of one of his shirt buttons.

Groans and escalated laughter from the game players prevented him from answering. He placed his forearm back across his eyes and shifted her till her head lay on his shoulder. Gradually she succumbed to the sleepiness pulling at her, where his face haunted her, smiling, serious and thoughtful.

She awoke when a little pistol named Abby climbed across her reaching for her precious Tonio.

Chapter 10

"Did you know that ancient kings would steal limbs off each other's mango trees so they could graft them into their own, to try and have the finest and best-tasting fruit? Even going so far as to bribe and kidnap the other king's gardeners?"

"No," Carina grunted as she swung a machete against the trunk of a young sapling, making a slit big enough to graft in a tiny proto-limb or bud from another variety of mango, a stronger, more durable type. Mingled with the sweeter version Don Rodriquez produced already, his harvest a few years down the road would weather the blights and infestations much better than what he had now. "I didn't know that. That's interesting."

"And do you know how the mango got its name?"

"No. Why don't you tell me?"

She held the bud in place as Juan Antonio wrapped the bottom of the tree in burlap, securing the grafted limb.

"Well, the mango was the most sold fruit in the world, although at one time the most horrible-tasting. But once the grafting technique became known and used, it produced the mango as we know it today. Man cannot and will not live without this fruit so he takes it with him. Wherever man goes, mangoes."

She stared at him then burst out laughing. "That was lame."

"Yes, but it worked."

"What do you mean?" She blinked so his image would focus clearly.

"You laughed, and your face lights up when you smile. I hoped it would take your mind off how tired you are."

She pressed both hands over her eyes as they burned with weariness. "I am exhausted, but so very happy we accomplished everything today. Don Rodriquez and his men can finish the grafting tomorrow. His orchard is healthy and has passed inspection, so guess what, Mr. Fuentes?"

"What, Miss Garza?"

"We're officially out of a job till we start on the Gonzales orchard."

"Verdad?"

"Yes, and I'm so glad. I want to help Marsha and April with VBS. Did you see what they did to the walls in Abby's class?"

Carina's church had only two Vacation Bible Schools in her childhood but she remembered them as very serious classes with Kool-Aid and cookies being the highlight of the evening. Abby's classroom wall had been painted a blue underwater ocean scene with a treasure chest at the bottom. All types of fish swam on the wall with seaweed and sand spilled along the base of the ocean. Delighted at what they had created, Carina had driven herself to finish work early. For some reason, she wanted to be a part of this VBS.

"I've never seen anything like it. They did the same thing last year, but it was a Hawaiian theme. They made leis for all the kids. I cut up the coffee straws."

Carina washed her hands under the outside faucet then splashed water on her face. She took the towel he handed her. "So do you attend church with the Garretts regularly?"

"If I'm here, I do. *Papi* knew the senior Garrets and introduced me. Rick Sr. officiated at *Papi*'s funeral."

"I'm sorry for your loss. Losing a parent is hard, I know. How long has it been?"

She watched him sluice water over his face and around the back of his neck. His brow furrowed and a muscle flickered in his jaw. He dried his face and hands before he answered, "A year ago, last month."

She touched his arm in sympathy and was abruptly caught by the elbow and gently forced into a run. She barely heard his words, "Last one to the truck has to drive," as he passed her up. Never one to refuse a challenge, she gave it all she had, arriving two seconds late, out of breath and wondering where the excess energy had come from. He dangled the keys in front of her, but when she reached for them, he held them above her head.

"I'll drive, but you have to talk and keep me awake."

"It's a deal."

Wearily she climbed into the truck seat and let the cool air conditioning waft over her. Thankfully they were only twenty-five minutes from Rick and Marsha's. She could hardly wait for a shower and food.

"Why did you cut up coffee straws?" The question niggled at the back of her mind but she'd forgotten to ask.

"We used fishing line to make the leis. I cut the straws into one-inch pieces as dividers between the flowers so the fishing line would not be seen."

"You're so clever. My hero." She sighed dramatically.

He reached for her hand and brought it to his lips. Happiness filled her. He had unlocked her heart and her soul.

"Tell me more about your family, Tonio." Her hand remained in his and lay on the console between them. "I know you have a mother and two brothers and that your father passed away. Do you have nieces and nephews?"

"No, neither brother is married. My mother lives six months in North Carolina and six months in South Texas."

There was a slight edge to his voice as if he didn't wish to speak of them, but Carina wanted to know all there was to know. Just being this close to him filled her with deep satisfaction.

"Why don't they live at the plantation with you?"

"They live in the States." He raised his hand from the steering wheel, exhaling with agitation. "I live in the States." His words were short and clipped. "Only my father lived in Mexico."

It troubled Carina that he seemed reluctant to open up to her. She sat in pained silence watching the sun drop off the horizon as dusk caused the need for headlights. She tried to ease her hand from underneath his but his grasp tightened.

"Carina, I've not had the best home life. My brothers are great, but the relationship with my mother has suffered majorly over the years. One day we'll talk about it because I want to share every part of me with you. To tell you the truth, it feels good. I don't want anything to hinder that."

He glanced briefly at her, his mouth curved with tenderness. That smile was not to be resisted.

"Are you scared?"

"To let you into my life? Absolutely not." He turned down the cobblestone street to the Garretts', stopping a short distance from the driveway. In the shadowy interior it was hard to see his expression. With a sense of awe and wonder she waited for his next words. She was not disappointed.

"What's happening between us is new and exciting. I can't wait to see you each morning and my last thoughts at night are of you. Watching you work and taking care of you feels like…" he paused as if searching for words "…like God has guided us into perfect harmony. It's monumental."

Without waiting for a response, he continued. "Sometimes I feel like I can send you my thoughts. When you answer and we're on the same wavelength…" He kissed the tips of his fingers. "Ah, sweet."

What he didn't say with words he said with his eyes. Happiness filled her. "It's the same for me. I have to see you every day. To feel you near, to hear your voice. Nothing like this has ever happened to me. I'm at a loss for what to do next. I just know I don't want it to stop."

He kissed the tip of her nose, then her forehead. Carina knew after the day of work she looked like a train wreck, but she still gloried in their moments together.

"What do we do next?" Her heart pounded, yet she felt a surreal calm.

He tipped her chin sideways and planted tiny kisses along her jawline. "What do you mean, *mi amor?*"

"Do we let people know we're an item?"

A deep chuckle greeted her question, his eyes sharp and assessing as he held her gaze. "I think we let things naturally take their course." His hand gently touched her shoulder then slid down her arm. With both her hands clasped in his he raised them to his lips. He kissed the backs then pressed a kiss in her palm before continuing, his thumb resting a moment on the rapid pulse in her wrist. "How could they not know when I can barely let you out of my sight?"

Juan Antonio lay awake long into the night, contemplating the events taking place in his life. His feet hung over the edge of the bottom bunk bed and the night-light burned too bright. None of that overly bothered him, but a certain green-eyed beauty held his thoughts captive. How had she become everything to him in just a few months? On the sofa last Sunday, he felt every breath she took in unison with his and he realized what they shared was sacred. It was the Biblical love that Ruth and Boaz, Abraham and Sarai had shared.

Carina was honest. She cared about others and had a talent for simple things that achieved great feats. The way she'd fought to save Don Diego's fruit after the way he'd treated her spoke of her character. She knew the Lord and had a love for His work. This growing need to hold her in his arms, to never let her out of his sight continually hammered at him like the tide against the shore outside his window. He could not stop himself from pondering what it would be like to have her with him all the time. To wake with her in his arms in the morning and whisper to her his last words at night.

Pensively, he stared out into the darkness. In his heart he knew she'd make an excellent mother, but would she love him enough? Quickly he banished the thought. There'd be time for those questions later. Her name lingered around the edges of his mind as he drifted off into a troubled sleep where images refused to focus but sounds of tears and arguments were the norm.

Chapter 11

Monday morning Carina climbed into the Suburban beside April and Marsha. Rick's parents, collected from the airport yesterday, were in front, Mr. Garrett driving and Abby and Caleb, the youngest Garrett children, in the very back. They were on their way to Llano Grande and the hot springs. Ms. Dottie claimed definite improvement in her arthritic joints from the water there and a bountiful picnic enticed the younger ones as well as a day away from the island.

Juan Antonio had left before daylight that morning to meet the real estate agent and show the hacienda to a prospective buyer.

As they bounced along the cobblestone streets, Carina wondered if she shouldn't have gone with him. Conversation was impossible, so she let her mind wander.

Yesterday, somewhat surprised at how young they

looked, Carina had shaken hands with Rick's parents, commenting on their youthful looks. The senior Garrets, in their early fifties, appeared to have no health problems at all. Mr. Garrett just last year had suffered a heart attack, yet to see him playing with the kids, one would never have suspected it. He swung Abby up in the air and round and round amid shrieks and giggling and pleas for release.

As the day wore on Carina could sense the excitement in the kids and even in Marsha at the Senior Garrets' presence. It took Carina a better part of the evening to analyze what she saw occurring. It was as if Rick and Marsha turned the reins over to the parents and became kids again. Marsha repeatedly asked Mrs. Garret, known by all as Ms. Dottie, what to do about things Carina herself had watched Marsha handle and handle well at that. Yet she heard Marsha ask what to do about the evening meal, the sleeping arrangements and if the theme for VBS was satisfactory to Miss Dottie.

Rick, too, appeared happy not to spend the evening studying, since his dad would preach the night service. Not that Mr. Garret Sr. had been asked; it just seemed to be standard procedure.

At Marsha's request, Carina had gone into the back yard to gather ripe fruit from the tree heavily loaded with green limes. She had the bowl almost full when she sensed she wasn't alone. She felt a smile tug her lips upward. The tantalizing smell of his aftershave preceded his surprise approach. An arm reached past her and shook the limb she was gathering from. Limes fell to the ground all around her.

"That's how it's done, city girl. If they fall from the limb, they're ripe."

Carina made no effort to retrieve the limes from the ground. She'd known all along to shake the tree, but hadn't wanted to collect the dirty ones from the ground. Choosing rather to ignore him, she turned to stalk back to the house. How long had he watched her stretch and pull at the limes, trying to get them off the branches before he offered his help? Even though she hadn't really needed his help, he couldn't know that.

Without warning a hand closed over her right shoulder. She looked up and her heart lurched madly. His compelling eyes riveted her to the spot, reminding her of the time she'd found him staring down at her from the second story of the hacienda. His voice when he spoke sounded deep and compassionate, captivating her even more than his dark eyes.

"Are you really upset with me, *amor,* or are you teasing me?" He pulled her into the shelter of his arm, whisking the bowl of limes from her grasp and setting them on the porch railing. He stepped in front of her and joined their hands together.

"Neither." She allowed a bit of sternness to enter her voice and narrowed her eyes at him. "I'm punishing you."

She all but chuckled aloud at his reaction. He paused, and seemed to mull her words over in his mind. She saw the uncertainty in his eyes and then determination squared his jaw and she knew then and there that he would let nothing stand between them. This was powerful stuff. A heady sensation caused her to inhale sharply. Her happiness was of utmost importance to him. She felt it down to her toes. She saw it in the dark eyes that never left hers for an instant. Until now, she hadn't realized that attraction was such a potent emotion.

"What have I done that you would need to punish me, *dulce* Carina?" When he pronounced her name *"Cah deen ah,"* she went a little weak in the knees. She looked down at their joined hands; the intensity of her feelings robbing her of speech. He was having none of it. With a gentle finger he lifted her chin, his expression still and serious.

She took a deep breath and adjusted her smile. "You watched me gathering those limes and all along you knew I was doing it wrong. Why didn't you show me the correct way sooner?" She allowed a teasing, accusatory tone to enter her voice. The relief in his expression was almost comical.

He pulled her to him in such a brief hug she wondered if she imagined it, then turned them to walk arm in arm around the house.

"First, I came looking for you because I cannot bear to be where you are not for any length of time. Secondly, the moment I saw you at the tree, I all but ran to help you, *amor,* because I wanted you to know the correct way to pick the limes. Like when you taught me how to wrap burlap around the grafting in the mango trees. It is the same, no?" His head swung lazily from side to side, a suspicious look entering his eyes. "Because I know a hard worker such as you wouldn't mind picking up the limes from the ground."

Well, how could she argue with that? Especially when she realized he had maneuvered them to the side of the house with no windows, creating privacy for the kiss she knew he intended to steal. He lowered his head and she felt his breath on her face.

"Whoa!" The Garrets' oldest son, Luke's, exclamation pulled them apart as he rounded the corner full steam ahead trying to escape his pursuers, three younger brothers intent on taking the ball from him and tackling him to the ground. "Sorry, dude." The curiosity in Luke's gaze caused a blush to spread over Carina's cheeks. Juan Antonio groaned. Her reaction seemed to amuse him then a momentary look of satisfaction crossed his features.

He whirled around and quickly plucked the ball from Luke's hands, tossed it over head to Seth and then ran for the invisible goal line. Effectively killing the curiosity cat.

Now this morning, riding with the family in the Suburban, Carina rallied to the present. She allowed a small smile to tug her mouth upward at the heart melting sensations provoked by such simple thoughts. She focused on the scene from the Suburban window and realized they were in the town of Acoponeta. What a contrast to Novillero. Even though the town was small compared to most city standards, it was joined, wall-to-wall stuccoed buildings. The only way to tell when a house ended and the neighboring house began was the color changed with each one. The houses were painted every color of the rainbow. Carina held tightly to the door's armrest as they were jostled against each other on the cobblestone street, majorly relieved when they drove onto a paved road.

Carina looked forward to the outing today as she would get to see a different part of Mexico. The hot springs, located halfway up the mountain, supposedly had shelter from prying eyes provided by huge bushes of bougainvillea and mesquite trees.

Many of the people on the island traveled up the mountain and gathered the mesquite limbs that fell from the trees, bundling them with twine, using them to cook fish and shrimp. They would dig a hole in the ground, put in the twigs of mesquite and when the wood burned down to red embers and smoke, they would lay the aluminum foil wrapped fish, shrimp and veggies in to cook. Carina had watched Don Diego cover the hole with a big piece of wood, closing in the smoke. The fish tasted of smoked mesquite and was delicious.

As they left Acoponeta the road became nothing more than a dirt track and Carina only thought she had been jostled before. Several times she felt her head hit the top of the auto. Marsha had one arm over the backseat trying unsuccessfully to hold Abby in place but even with the aid of seat belts the two children were tossed up, down and sideways. But the shrieks and laughter assured the other occupants that the kids were enjoying every moment.

After twenty minutes Carina was sure she'd have bruises on her arms from being thrown roughly against the door. She breathed a sigh of relief when Mr. Garrett pulled off the side of the road into a small overlook big enough for two cars. She opened her door and then screamed. April grabbed her, securely holding her in her seat. Had she exited the vehicle she'd have fallen down a steep embankment, most likely crippling her or even killing her.

"Well, ladies, I guess we'll get out on the other side." Mr. Garret's calm statement set the others in motion but a sense of foreboding crossed the corridors of Carina's mind. The Garrets knew this area like the back of their hands but it would serve her well to stick close to them to prevent any unforeseen dangers.

Everyone carried a backpack or basket and they followed Mr. Garret into the shrubs on the opposite side of the road. Fifteen minutes later they arrived at the springs and excitement zinged through Carina. Steam rose from the water nestled in a small natural pool, not much bigger than the fish ponds people had begun putting in their yards back in the States.

Without any prior warning, Caleb grabbed his knees and did a backflip into the water. Carina sucked in a deep breath but when she heard Marsha laugh she realized he'd done this before. Mr. Garrett had already set the cooler with drinks on a makeshift table and quickly removed his shoes and socks. Everyone had brought a change of clothes, but looking around, Carina wondered where they could undress with privacy, and then Ms. Dottie walked into the water, fully clothed. *Ahh, so that's it. We put the change of clothing on when we get out.*

Everyone went into the water, Marsha holding Abby because the water appeared over her head. Carina sat on a rock watching. She couldn't help the caution screaming in her head; the place looked like a snake-infested den.

"Hey, have you guys heard of the two-step snake?" Carina deliberately kept her voice casual as she checked around the edges of the rock she was sitting on.

"Yeah. If it bites you you're dead before you take two steps," Mr. Garrett answered with staid calmness. Carina briefly wondered what might excite him.

"So…" She didn't want to be a spoilsport but snakes terrified her. She didn't have to deal with them in her

line of work because the orchards were kept clean of
grass and weeds that could steal nutrients from the
trees. No weeds to hide in equaled no snakes. But this
was like a jungle. "It doesn't give you the creeps to be
under these hanging vines and surrounded by shrubs?"

"Nope." Irked by his cool, aloof manner, Carina slid
off the rock and tiptoed through the undercover brush.
Reaching the pool she hurried in then gasped at the heat
of the water. Just as quickly her body adjusted and she
fought an overwhelming desire to lay her head against
the bank for a nap. "Two-steps are in the Amazon, not
in Mexico."

Nice of him to finally enlighten us.

Marsha placed Abby at the edge of the pool where
the water emptied into a stream and was considerably
cooler. She returned to the middle close to April and sat
in the water with only her head exposed. Carina cop-
ied her movements.

"Exactly what is this supposed to do for you?" The
water had lulled her into such a relaxed mood her voice
sounded barely above a whisper. No one else spoke,
splashed about, or moved for that matter.

Marsha moved to more shallow water then leaned
back on her elbows. "Well, it's proven to help arthritis,
rheumatism, skin diseases. I can't vouch for any of that
but Ms. Dottie says it helps her arthritis for up to three
months or so and she doesn't have to take much medi-
cine during that time. And Seth had ringworm once
and we brought him here. Within a week it healed up,
so we credited it to the water." She leaned forward, lifting her chin to keep her face from being submerged. "I
don't really care if the waters heal or not. I just like the

relaxation. This is my spa day." Marsha laughed softly, seemingly reluctant to disturb the ambience of the place.

Carina thought of her mother and how arthritis had formed small knots on her fingers causing her difficulty in opening things. She wished she could bring her here. Simply on the chance the hot water would numb the pain for a while. She wondered what her mother was doing at the moment. She missed her suddenly and wished she could explain the delightful things happening to her and Juan Antonio.

Lost in thought, Carina became aware of her surroundings at Marsha's gasp. The deceptively calm authority in her voice when she requested Caleb bring Abby to her caused Carina to take a quick look around. Her blood chilled.

Standing on the bank were ten or twelve men dressed in dark green camouflage uniforms. To an inexperienced eye, they appeared to be soldiers; but the black bandannas around their heads and the weapons they carried identified them as part of the most dreaded group in Mexico. Drug cartel.

Chapter 12

Not good. Not good at all. She turned to face them, easing closer to Marsha. The hot water did not stop the shiver of panic that shook her body. Fearful images built in her mind. With a crazy mixture of hope and fear she looked at Mr. Garrett. His calm nature would come in handy right about now. Where was he? She quickly scanned the area behind her. Not in sight. Marsha's hand gripped her leg under the water. Her whispered "Sit still" did little to quiet Carina's spasmodic trembling. She became increasingly uneasy under the silent scrutiny of the men watching them. The water's heat, which just moments before had soothed tired muscles and stiff joints, now seemed to scorch her skin. Sweat broke out across her forehead.

One of the men searched through the backpacks, scattering their personal belongings on the ground.

He shook his head at the man who appeared to be the leader. The leader walked to the water's edge and motioned them to get out. Drenched and with her shirt clinging to her, Carina followed the others.

"Donde estan las llaves?" The words cut the silence, his voice cold and exact.

Marsha pointed to the first bag the man ransacked then answered in English. "The keys are in the side pocket."

Her reply seemed to spark anger in the man who searched the bags. But watching him closely, Carina thought she saw a shimmer of fear in his eyes. She wondered what would happen to him when the keys were found. Would he be punished for making a mistake?

But at his triumphant *"Ja"* and turning the pocket inside out, the leader turned to Marsha and slapped her hard across the face. She fell sideways onto her knees. Abby screamed and cried, clutching at her mother. Marsha quickly shushed her and gathered her close. Carina reached out, intending to help her to her feet, but someone grabbed her by her hair, pulling her away. The force of the man's grip held her upright, her head back, chin out. Pain sliced through her brow. Tears filled her eyes but she blinked them away. Some inner voice whispered that it wasn't a good idea to show fear.

No sooner had that thought entered her mind, than Marsha stood, with Abby clinging to her legs. Carina recognized Marsha's deliberate refusal to pick up her child as a protective measure. Who knew what they would do to her if the keys weren't found. Carina tried to turn her head for a glimpse of the others. The only one she could see was Caleb, and tears ran silently down his cheeks and fear, stark and vivid, glittered in his young eyes. Six-year-olds should never have to face circumstances this dire.

Anger surged through her and she jerked her head forward. Whether she surprised her captor or not, she'd never know. He released her. She held a trembling hand out to Caleb. He rushed to her side and buried his head against her wet shirt. For a moment no one moved.

The leader addressed Marsha again. *"Donde estan las llaves?"* She stared back with little evident fear; only the tremble in her hand as she rubbed Abby's hair gave her away.

Once again she answered him in English. "I thought I put them in the side pocket." She patted her pockets but everyone could see there was no key bulge. She pointed to the water. "May I?" The leader nodded and stepped aside allowing her to enter the springs again. Marsha walked to where she'd been sitting and knelt on her knees feeling along the bottom of the springs. Her movements became almost frantic and she covered every inch of the small pool. Finally, she stood with her head bowed, her shoulders slumped in defeat.

The tension visibly increased among the small group gathered on the bank as the leader motioned Marsha from the water. Carina watched the muscles of his forearm harden beneath his sleeve as he roughly pulled Marsha up the bank then shoved her to the ground at Carina's feet.

"Loca mujeres. Give us the keys and we will not harm you."

Carina had read hundreds of newspaper accounts of kidnappings for ransom, beheadings, burying bodies in sand and setting the shoulders and heads on fire, but the one constant in Mexico's drug war was auto theft. The cartel wanted vehicles that would not raise suspicion. Family cars or all-terrain vehicles. If they took the Suburban maybe they really would leave them alone. She quickly knelt beside Marsha. "Where are the keys, Marsha? If we give them to these men they will let us go."

"Shush, Carina. Don't appear to be on their side." Marsha covered her whispered words by attempting to rise. A gun pressed to the side of her head and she sank back to the ground, her eyes lifting to Carina in mute appeal.

Carina jerked to her feet. She breathed in shallow, quick gasps. She needed a moment to think. Her actions had brought a gun to Marsha's head, not what she'd intended. She glanced toward the others in their group. Ms. Dottie leaned heavily against April's side and Abby, who had gone to April when her mother went into the water, clutched her leg. Caleb's hand still gripped the edges of Carina's culottes. Only Marsha lacked the comforting touch of a loved one.

The men huddled together, speaking purposefully in low undertones. Carina strained to catch what they said. Two men left the group, walking toward where they'd left the Suburban. Carina's troubled spirits quieted. Mr. Garret must have left the keys in the ignition. Those men would find them, then take the car and go. Suddenly a quick and disturbing thought entered her mind and she gasped. Where was Mr. Garrett? She glanced at Marsha, the question on the tip of her tongue. Just then, Ms. Dottie slipped to the ground in a faint.

"Mama?" April's anguished cry rent the air. The drug leader rushed to her side, a curse on his lips. April ignored him. She eased her mother's head onto her lap, pushing hair back from her forehead. She gave Ms. Dottie a little shake. "Mom, wake up." Tears streamed down her cheeks. Abby wailed loudly and the leader grabbed her by both wrists and swung her toward Marsha.

"Shut that child up, now!" he growled.

Marsha swept Abby into her arms, a cry of protest dying on her lips as she gathered her precious daughter close to her heart.

The leader knelt beside Ms. Dottie and felt for the pulse in her neck. He cocked his gun and put it to her head. April screamed. Marsha started forward and Carina sank to the ground, a prayer tumbling from her lips. "Dear God. Help us." Amazingly, Ms. Dottie's eyes opened. She muttered something and struggled to sit up.

The leader stood. His mouth took on an unpleasant twist and a frown settled on his features. His eyes weighed Marsha with a critical squint as he addressed her in Spanish.

"We are moving to a new location. I will not tolerate any more of this nonsense. You keep up with us or we shoot you. *Comprende?*"

"Sí, comprende." For the first time, Marsha answered him in Spanish.

Carina began the trek up the side of the mountain, holding Caleb's hand, falling in behind Marsha, who carried Abby and was first in line. Arm in arm, April and Ms. Dottie brought up the rear with several guards spread out in intervals between them.

A Bible verse flitted through her mind. *"What time I am afraid, I will trust in thee." Lord, I'm afraid and I have no one else to trust in. I'm trusting in You.* She thought through several scenarios, remembering stories from early school days where captives broke off tree limbs so rescuers could easily track them. She tried to break a tiny limb from a shrub, but it held firm. She had nothing on her person to drop along the trail. *Lord, please,* her heart cried, *show me what to do.*

Carina's flip-flop caught on a root and she stumbled. Grabbing Caleb's shoulder to steady herself, she suddenly realized she was the only one in their group who wore shoes. The rest had gone barefoot into the hot springs, but she'd been afraid of foreign critters and had kept her shoes on. "Caleb, here." She reached for one of her shoes. "Put these on so you won't get burs on your feet."

"No." The handle of a gun was shoved into her back and she shrieked. "You wear shoes."

Black eyes stared at her from a bandanna-covered face. The man made no other move, but as she stared at him, he lowered his gaze. With the butt of his gun he motioned them forward. What was going on here? He seemed ashamed at the circumstances. Maybe she could work on him. Soften him somehow. She glanced back to familiarize herself with his attire or any identifying difference between him and his dressed-alike comrades. He placed a hand on his hip and she found her mark. A cell phone clipped to his belt stood out strangely in comparison with the other equipment. Not just any phone but a new-model iPhone if she wasn't mistaken. Interesting. She needed to check if the others had similar new phones.

They arrived at a clearing and the leader signaled for them to stop. Marsha sank to the ground, Abby still in her arms. The others followed suit, but Carina remained standing. She looked for the man with the phone but he'd vanished. How odd.

Marsha patted the ground beside her. "Come sit with me, Carina."

Carina eased down, eager to share her thoughts with the others. "Did you notice the guy behind me and Caleb? He had a new cell phone on his belt and he seemed sympathetic to us." Excitedly she tried to offer the Garretts hope.

"Keep your voice down. Don't look directly at them and when they approach stare at their chest, never their eyes." Marsha spoke with quiet emphasis.

Carina lowered her voice but increased the intensity. "But what if there's a way we can get through to him? Maybe offer reward money for letting us go."

"Carina, please," April exclaimed with a twinge of annoyance. "You'll get us killed if you're not careful."

"That's exactly what will happen if we do nothing." Carina tried to calm the irritation she heard in her voice, but fear and anger battled inside her. To give up went against her American spirit.

"Carina?" Ms. Dottie scooted closer and took Carina's hand. Her touch was reassuring, her voice calm. "We haven't given up. We've worked the situation from the beginning. We just haven't revealed our game plan."

Carina raised her eyes to find Ms. Dottie watching her. Almost as if willing her to understand. Her mind reviewed the past hour for signs of strategic planning and came up with nothing. The only thing she wanted to know was where Mr. Garrett had disappeared to and why the women hadn't mentioned him. Her eyes widened.

"Mr. Garrett…"

"Exactly." Ms. Dottie nodded. "They have no clue that a member of our party is missing and has most likely gone for help." She patted Carina's hand. "My little fainting spell took your mind right off his absence, didn't it?"

"You mean you staged that?"

"You were about to blurt out that he had the keys, right? I couldn't let that happen as he was our only hope of escape."

"Silencio!"

Carina hadn't seen the guard approach. She gasped, a shiver of panic racing through her. Had he heard their conversation? Did the guards understand English? When he walked away she exhaled a long sigh.

She shifted on the hard ground, trying to relax.

"Let's sit with our backs together for support." Marsha whispered the words while her eyes never left the guards hovering together in discussion. Ms. Dottie positioned her back against April and Carina leaned against Marsha. The relief was immediate. She pulled Caleb to her side. Abby sat on her mother's lap.

The guards seemed to be in a heated discussion, yet Carina could not piece together the few words she caught.

"Mama, can I have a drink of water?" The whine in Abby's voice echoed Carina's own stifled feelings. Tired, hot and thirsty and feeling unusually weak. What was up with that?

"Not right now, Abby. Be a big girl for Mama, okay?" Marsha pulled Abby closer. "How are you feeling, Ms. Dottie? You okay?"

Carina glanced sideways at Ms. Dottie and exclaimed in dismay, "Ms. Dottie, what's wrong?"

"Shh, keep your voice down. I may be a little dehydrated. We left our bottled water by the springs. Then the long trek up the mountain…well, it seems to be taking its toll." The hand she placed against her forehead shook and her face blanched.

"Dehydration. That's why I feel so funny. Let's ask for water." Carina started to rise but Ms. Dottie stopped her with a strong grip on her arm.

"You'll do no such thing. Sit still. Any move you make right now could get us killed."

"We can't just sit here and do nothing."

"We can and we will." Ms. Dottie spoke in a broken whisper, her voice resigned. "Pray, Carina. Pray like you've never prayed before."

Chapter 13

Juan Antonio closed the hacienda door, his mood buoyant over the agent's words. The prospective buyers had placed ten thousand dollars earnest money in escrow so no one else could buy the home till they secured a loan. His goal was within sight. He would finally be free to pursue his dream.

That dream might include Carina. He'd quit trying to deny she was more to him than a casual acquaintance. Yet how could he forget she also represented the things he disliked in a woman? She was good at her job. He had to admit that; and she made him happy. For now. But he knew too well the heartache caused by constant separation required by a career like hers. Perhaps he could convince her to give up her job for him. In the name of love.

Carina did not give up easily. He'd come to realize that about her. So where did that leave them? If he wasn't careful, he'd end up just like his dad: alone and heartbroken, with nothing but an old hacienda and an orchard full of mangos.

Right now though, anything seemed possible. The hacienda would soon be off his hands. He'd have funds to buy seed for sugarcane. His brothers could repair and purchase new equipment for their individual places. He was young and strong and the world was his oyster.

He landed the plane on the beach and cut the motor. He was about to see Carina. He determined in his heart not to reveal his joy at seeing her. That even his walk had a sunny cheerfulness failed to register, and if his heart sang with delight as he opened the Garrets' back door, then it must be because life was good.

That was before he saw the look on Rick's face and noticed the tears on Seth's cheeks.

"What's up, guys?" He addressed Luke, the elder of Rick's sons.

"They burned the car," Seth blurted out.

"They're missing." Jonathan's voice held a faint thread of hysteria, his blue eyes full of pain.

Swallowing down a sudden uneasiness, he turned to Rick. "What are they talking about?"

"The rest of the crowd left this morning for the hot springs in Acoponeta. They should have been back by lunch. They didn't return. I figured they were shopping, having a good time, but Alfredo sent a message that a Suburban like mine had been burned at the springs. We called the police but have heard nothing." Rick ran a hand harshly through his hair. He just as quickly smoothed it down. Indecision marked his every move.

Juan Antonio spoke through the talon of fear clawing at his throat. "Carina?"

"She's with them."

"Let's go." No way on earth could Juan Antonio sit and wait for them to bring him news. He had to be there, had to find her. Them.

"Someone has to man the post here," Rick began.

"Luke is a man now. He knows how to contact us if they should arrive back here or if word comes from the police. Right, Luke?" Juan Antonio watched the battle war across his young friend's face and knew the inner turmoil he must feel. To stay meant he might not be there to help should the family need rescuing, but to go left the contact post unmanned. Juan Antonio knew the decision had been made when Luke clenched his jaw and nodded.

"I'll stay." His lips pressed shut as if fearful he might cry.

Rick jumped into action. He touched the shoulders of his two younger sons. "Jonathan, you and Seth stay with him. Keep an eye out for strange vehicles that might leave a message in the yard or at the door. Gather as much information as you can. What model, color. Keep the door locked. Don't let anyone in. You have our numbers. Call till you reach one of us. Understand?" At their solemn nods, he continued. "Right now, though, we need flashlights, matches, water..." He paused. "First we need to pray."

Rick knelt by a kitchen chair and the boys followed suit. Juan Antonio tried to disguise his annoyance at the delay. When Rick and his sons all began to pray at once, Juan Antonio knelt in shame. He heard the anxiety in their voices, the fear and the dread. He placed his head on his arm and added his pleas to theirs. "Lord, please let no harm come to our loved ones. Answer the prayers of these kids and Rick. And God, if You choose to hear me, please keep Carina safe."

When Juan Antonio stood, Rick had his sons in a bear hug, all three reaching their arms around their dad, unashamed of the tears that rolled down their faces. Juan Antonio felt bereft. He had loved his dad, still loved his brothers, but what would it feel like to have sons wrap their arms around him in love?

In minutes they had the truck loaded and were headed toward the hot springs. Thirty minutes later they drove as close as allowed to the flashing lights of the *policia*. When Rick identified himself as the owner of the burned vehicle, they were led beyond the police barrier to the chief. He informed them that the vehicle held no occupants when the fire consumed it, that they'd found no one at the hot springs and that there had not been anyone there since around eleven that morning. Other than the burned car there was no evidence of foul play.

"And the missing persons? That's not evidence of foul play?" Rick's voice was quiet, yet held an undertone of cold contempt. Juan Antonio studied his friend carefully. He'd never known Rick to be anything but friendly and kind. He turned to observe the chief's reaction to the obvious contempt in Rick's voice. The man's lids lowered for a moment and when he looked up again his eyes blazed with anger.

"Perhaps you should tell me how many are missing." Drops of moisture clung to the man's forehead, and his nostrils flared in anger.

This would not do. Antonio had no idea what lay between his friend and this police chief, but he would not allow it to hinder the investigation into where Carina had gone. He purposely took charge of the conversation.

"Sir, there is one man, four women and two children missing. They came to the springs early this morning and planned to return to Novillero by lunch today. They still have not shown up."

The chief looked at his watch. "So they've officially been missing around seven hours."

"Right."

"They could be anywhere." He looked over at the burned vehicle. "Is anyone at home, and can they contact you should the missing show up?"

"Yes, we left Rick's teenage son in charge and there are two others with him." Juan Antonio didn't add that they were underage children. However, the boys were mature for their age and had loads of common sense, thanks to great parenting.

An argument broke out between several officers behind the chief and he excused himself to join his men. A heated discussion ensued and Juan Antonio moved closer to see what was going on. Rick stopped him with a hand on his arm.

"That's a corrupt officer. Don't be fooled by anything he says."

Juan Antonio trusted Rick's opinions explicitly, but under the circumstances he needed to know the reason for the caution. "What makes you say that?"

"When we built the youth camp on the beach a church back east donated several stoves, refrigerators and sinks. We drove to the border to pick them up and brought them here in Dad's cargo trailer. Zuniga there—" he nodded toward the chief "—confiscated them and charged us two thousand dollars to release them. Said we failed to pay duty on them when we crossed the border in Texas. Not only did we pay duty, we gave him the receipt. He lied and said we had no receipt. He made us pay in cash. He pocketed the money, smiled in our faces. He knew we had no other recourse than what he dealt us. I don't trust him not to be a part of this somehow."

"That's all we need in this situation. A corrupt cop." A flicker of anxiety swept through him. To alienate this man could shatter the only thread of expertise they had. But to be deceived by him could mean the death of Rick's family and Carina. They needed a common ground. "Do you think he's holding them for ransom?" The undeniable and dreadful facts sank deep into his heart. Carina had family in the States. Possibly wealthy. This man may have investigated her from day one. They could demand a ransom from her family and once paid, they would kill the hostages.

"Right now I don't know what to think. But in another hour or so the sun will set and we'll lose any signs to follow. God help us. If it rains during the night we're doomed."

"Then let's go. We don't have to wait." Juan Antonio felt rather than saw Rick fall in behind him as they started to the springs.

"*Esperate*. Halt! Where do you think you're going?" The chief all but ran to catch up with them.

"We're burning daylight, Zuniga. I'm going to find my family." Rick's profile was strong and rigid, and Juan Antonio would not have dared tangle with him at that moment. The chief, however, had no such reservations.

"You must not interfere. The evidence will be destroyed. I can't allow it."

"We're going." Rick towered over the chief and his officers by a full eight inches and one look into his flat, hard eyes had the chief stammering like a rookie.

"Then you walk behind us and follow our orders, *comprende?*"

"Sí, comprende."

Rick walked to his truck and removed two backpacks. He handed one to Juan Antonio and fit his arms through the other. Surprised at the weight, Juan Antonio did likewise and set out after the others.

At the springs, they found personal belongings: backpacks, totes, even Carina's purse and passport. Alarm bells rang in Juan Antonio's mind. This was no ordinary robbery or they'd have taken the money and her passport. In his heart, he'd held on to hope that they'd show up at home. The boys would call and say all was well. Sinking despair increased by the minute. He searched for a plausible explanation to their disappearance. Drug cartel mostly robbed or killed for money or to make a statement. The money had been left behind, not much assuredly, but three hundred dollars was nothing to sneeze at.

Since no one in the group was wealthy, unless Carina possessed wealth he didn't know about, none had ties to the government or were part of a vendetta. So why had they been kidnapped?

"Look." Rick pointed to the opposite bank. "Those are boot heels. Everyone's shoes are here this side of the springs."

"But there are no tracks other than the boots, so they

didn't leave the springs in that direction." The chief offered tentatively, still uneasy with Rick's presence.

Rick climbed the bank, careful not to disturb the boot prints. He stood perfectly still, studying the terrain, then finally motioned for the chief to join him. Juan Antonio joined them and there in the midst of many boot tracks, was a tiny woven mark with ridges that looked like the sole of a tennis shoe. Excitedly they found the next print and began to track their way up the mountain.

Dusk settled between the trees and they turned on flashlights. An hour later the chief called a halt to the search, stating tiredness would cause mistakes.

"Really? You're stopping?" Juan Antonio could not keep the sarcasm from his voice. "We've been at this all of forty-five minutes. They have eight hours on us. We can't stop now."

The chief looked at Rick and answered, completely ignoring Juan Antonio. It annoyed him to no end.

"We're making too much noise. We could stumble right into an ambush. If this is cartel they may kill one of the hostages as a warning. Is that what you want?" He gave a tight-lipped smile at Rick's negative response. "I didn't think so."

"You and your men may stay here, but Juan Antonio and I will continue. We'll be quiet and keep our eyes open. I can't let my family die without doing everything in my power to find them."

Rick's cell phone rang, startling them in the semi-darkness. He answered it quickly only to tell the boys their family hadn't been found.

"You see what I mean, Señor Garrett?" The chief smiled without humor. "You would have given us away, placed us in danger. You need to go home and care for your family there. Leave the investigation to the *policia*."

Rick muted his phone as did Juan Antonio. "Is there anything you'd like to share with us that might help?" Rick shifted the backpack to a more comfortable position while staring at the chief. The man realized he was fighting a losing battle. Juan Antonio wondered briefly if he and Rick weren't playing right into enemy hands. Why else would Mexican police allow a gringo and himself to aid in an obvious crime investigation?

"Don't talk. Keep your lights low to the ground with minimal movement. Walk lightly and extinguish your light often and listen, perhaps fifteen minutes or more each time." He studied them intensely. "If you find them, observe, but do not let your presence be known. You have no weapons. They will be heavily armed and they enjoy killing. You will serve as front men. Gather facts, and when we arrive, stay out of the line of fire. What good will it do your family if you get yourself killed?"

Two hours later, Juan Antonio froze into silence. He didn't move or breathe. Someone was moving stealthily down the mountain, headed straight at him.

Chapter 14

Just like the darkness that settled round them, Carina's mind filled with dread as she lay on the hard ground. A terrifying realization washed over her. She might die. And if she did, she'd never get to tell Juan Antonio just how much she loved him. Oh, yes, she knew with startling certainty her heart belonged to him. She would never forget a single detail of his face; those dark eyes that showed intelligence and independence of spirit. The square jaw and straight nose, and the whiteness of his smile that contrasted pleasingly with his olive skin. She thought of his teasing laughter when she shared her taquito with him that first morning at the hacienda.

She understood now that he'd protected her from Don Diego when he confronted him at breakfast after learning the man tried to scare her away. The memory brought a wry, twisted smile to her face. She'd argued with him, then sprayed him with water. What a humiliating, deflating feeling even now. They'd gotten past it, though, and she recalled the breathless feeling at being enclosed in his strong arms at the lime tree. She stifled a sob.

She felt Marsha reach for her hand.

"You're thinking about Tonio?" Marsha's ability to zero in on her thoughts never ceased to amaze Carina.

"Yes," she whispered back.

"You love him?"

It was pointless to deny it. With a flash of wild grief she answered, "Yes."

"How wonderful."

Tears choked her. She gulped hard. "I may never get to tell him."

"I'm sure he already knows."

"Do you think they're looking for us?"

Marsha shifted to lay Abby on the ground and sat up. Carina propped on her elbow. "If I know Rick Garret, and I do, he's on his way to us right now. I pray he doesn't get himself killed. He can be such a hothead at times."

"It's always over you or the kids, though, because he loves you so much." Unaware that April was listening, Carina was startled by her reply.

"So you guys are not worried? You think we're gonna make it out of this?"

"We can't be sure of that, but if we die it will still be okay. We're ready to meet the Lord and though I've no desire to leave my family, if that's God's will then that will be what's best." Marsha sounded as if she meant every word.

"How could that be what's best? What a senseless

loss to the people in Novillero. Surely the Lord would rather you continue being a missionary. Look at all you've done for Him, the sacrifices you've made."

"But everything we've done, been given or even accomplished is nothing but for Christ."

April spoke quietly. *"But what things were gain to me those I counted loss for Christ."*

Carina felt poleaxed. April quoted the verse that had been in Carina's devotions the very day April had arrived. The verse Carina had wondered about. Caught off guard by the sudden clarity of the verse, she sat up wide awake. "So you're saying all that you are and have belong to Christ. He can have everything back because you just want Him?"

"Right. We have nothing more important than Him. Nothing we accomplish can ever repay what He did for us on Calvary. So whatever He wills for our lives will be fine." Marsha responded with conviction in her voice.

"Even if you die? Or, God forbid, one of your children?"

Marsha did not hesitate even for a moment. "Even death." Carina heard her swallow and knew the conversation proved difficult. "Not that any of this is easy to accept, but my confidence is in Him. I know He loves me and I know He hears my prayers. What He allows to happen will be in my best interest."

Carina felt the tears roll down her face. Not tears of fear, but tears of joy that God had personally shown her the true meaning of a scripture passage. She felt blessed beyond measure and suddenly she, too, knew that it would be all right. Whatever the outcome, she would love the Lord.

She lay again on the hard earth and fell into sweet

slumber only to awaken thirty or forty minutes later to bright lights and commotion. Two guards shoved someone to the ground then delivered a hard kick to the abdomen. The man doubled up clutching his stomach, turning sideways to face them. She registered Ms. Dottie's cry even as she identified the bruised and battered Mr. Garret Sr.

Juan Antonio felt behind him, trying to gauge the distance between himself and Rick. Rick clasped his arm, pulling sideways out of the path of the oncoming intruder. Before he could move, the running stopped, followed by a thud and a moan. A light flashed on, and his brow rose in astonishment. Before him two guards had forced a man to the ground. They yanked his head up by his hair, and Juan Antonio stared into the eyes of Rick's dad. Rick pressed forward but Juan Antonio held him back. He'd seen what Rick had not; a negative shake of the head from the senior Mr. Garrett.

By some twist of fate, or by the hand of God, they were hidden behind shrubs and the limb of a mesquite tree. Here was their main piece of evidence. Stealthily they tracked the men back to where they'd camped, staying far enough behind that their footsteps weren't heard over those in front of them. How Rick watched them kick his dad and not rush to the rescue, Juan Antonio would never know, because it took teeth-grinding restraint to keep from doing so himself.

He could see Carina and the others beyond the shadow of the flashlight and relief swept through him. They were alive. Now if Mr. Garrett would remain calm, the *policia* would arrive after daybreak and arrest these criminals.

The guards joined those who had been sleeping near the edge of the clearing. Something tugged at Juan Antonio's memory. A television program about border wars had stated that the cartel never held hostages long; killing or cutting them loose was the norm. It also stated hostages were always tied, blindfolded and gagged.

He studied the position of the guards and the distance between them and the hostages. Something didn't add up. These men acted like amateurs. The women could easily have escaped while the two guards chased Mr. Garrett.

He watched Ms. Dottie crawl close to her husband and take his head in her lap. His right arm slid around her waist, his left he kept hugged to his body. Juan Antonio longed to walk over and take Carina in his arms. He would never let her go.

The gray light of dawn crept slowly through the trees as Juan Antonio stood, careful to make no sound as he stretched the kinks from his neck and shoulders. His eyes felt like he'd been in a desert sandstorm, his legs numb from the cramped position he'd assumed through the night.

Without a whisper of noise, he turned to find Rick beside him, pointing at his watch. Chief Zuniga should arrive within the hour if he left as early as he promised.

Before either of them could blink, six men dressed from head to toe in fatigues and headgear, and carrying automatic rifles, walked to the sleeping men and nudged them awake with their guns. He and Rick saw the fright and then resignation in the men's eyes as they realized they'd been beaten. The question that sent a chill down Juan Antonio's spine was, by whom? These men were not Chief Zuniga's. They looked like United States Army personnel.

One of the guards on the ground wearing a modern cell phone on his side stood and bumped fists with the six new guys. So was he undercover? The man then woke the ladies before kneeling to check Mr. Garret's injuries.

On his feet again he looked directly to the spot Juan Antonio and Rick were hiding. "You can come out, guys."

Juan Antonio looked at Rick but Rick wasted no time getting to his family. Juan Antonio followed a bit slower, still uncertain who these rescuers were. But when Carina ran to him, he forgot everything else. She flung her arms around his neck; his arms encircled her, hands locked against her spine. She buried her face against his throat and he whispered her name, a groan escaping at his near loss.

He drew back to see her face. He needed a kiss like a man needs air to breathe. Weariness deepened the shadows under her eyes, which were ringed with dark circles, but she was the most beautiful woman he'd ever seen. He brushed a kiss across her forehead, then gently covered her mouth. He drank in the comfort of her nearness. He could wait no longer. He eased her away and tipped her chin up so he could watch her response. "I love you, Carina."

Tears filled her eyes, but a smile broadened in approval and joy shone in her eyes. "I love you, too, Juan Antonio Fuentes. With all my heart."

She settled against him, her head a perfect fit beneath his chin. He never wanted to let her go. She belonged to him.

"Juan Antonio." Rick's voice called him from the side. "These officers want to speak with us."

Carina listened to the report from the officers, her mind in a fog. It had not been drug cartel, but Don Diego extracting revenge on her. Because of her, she'd nearly gotten her friends killed. As the story unfolded, the Mexican *Federales* had been investigating Don Diego for several years. His ties to the Mexican Mafia had sent up red flags. They sent one of their own to infiltrate his compound. To Carina's amazement it was the cell phone guy. But he'd almost hit her with his gun and had forced her to wear her shoes.

She looked at him in disbelief. He noticed her apparent observation and enlightened her. "You were the only one with shoes and the only one leaving tracks for my men to follow. A lighter person like this young man—" he patted Caleb's shoulder "—would have put no pressure on the shoes, thereby leaving no tracks." A cheeky grin preceded his next words. "Sorry if I offended, ma'am."

"Not a problem, sir."

Juan Antonio held out his hand. "Thank you so much for what you've done. For saving the lives of our loved ones."

"Just doing my job."

The Garrets added their thanks, including the senior Garret, who was able to stand and walk unaided.

Amid all the thank-yous and handcuffing prisoners, Chief Zuniga and his *policia* arrived. They tried to claim the prisoners as theirs but the *Federales* were having none of it.

Trembling with relief, Carina followed Juan Antonio down the mountain, his tender ministrations going a long way toward easing the guilt consuming her.

When they reached the burned Suburban, she lost control. The reality of how close they had come to death chilled her and sobs tore from her throat. Juan Antonio gathered her almost roughly against him, but she'd already glimpsed the moisture in his own eyes.

She felt a hand on her shoulder and turned to Marsha's embrace and they cried together till calm began to settle within them.

Slowly she let her gaze rest on each person in the little group. She found only love gazing back, acceptance and relief. She would never forget this family, but if God would allow it, she would return to Texas the second she completed her assignment. She wanted her mother and she wanted safety. She would kiss the ground of her beloved United States. She'd had enough of her father's homeland to last her a lifetime.

Chapter 15

The Garrets began Vacation Bible School the next week and Carina marveled at the lack of concern they demonstrated over the kidnapping. She, on the other hand, was a wreck. She looked in the closets at night, under the bed and refused to go anywhere alone. The only good things in her life were her relationships with God and Juan Antonio.

Seems he seldom left her side, even helping in her class during VBS. She'd never felt so complete in her life.

"Hello, beautiful lady." She smiled as his arm slid around her waist, loving even the smell of him. "What are you making?"

The Garrets' kitchen had been turned into a craft room, piled high with the things they couldn't take to church until needed. She held up the sandwich bag clasped in the middle with pipe cleaners. On one side of the bag were little fish snacks, the opposite side filled with grapes. The pipe cleaners curled at the end and with eyes added to the bag it looked like a butterfly. "This is tonight's VBS snack."

"Such talent in those little hands." He landed a kiss near her ear and sent her stomach into a wild swirl.

"Tonight is the last night of VBS." He took her hands in his. "Will you go on a date with me tomorrow night? Just the two of us, somewhere special?" He placed her hands against his, comparing the differences in size.

"Yes, yes, yes." She interspersed each word with a light kiss. "There's nothing I enjoy more than spending time with you."

His dark eyes glowed happiness and she felt woozy with power that she was responsible. Surely he felt the same. She could not get enough of his presence. If he left a room she found herself following. If she left, she looked up and there he'd be.

"Good. We'll leave around four and fly to Mazatlan, okay?" He brushed a ribbon of hair over her shoulder, his hand lingering a moment against her cheek. "If this is what Joseph felt for Mary, it's no wonder he willingly married her and her with a child not his."

"I think maybe the angel might have had something to do with that," Carina teased.

"I'm counting on the angels helping me, too."

"You don't need angels. I'm yours. I only want to be with you. I love you so much."

"Ah, Carina, you complete me. This is madness. I can't stay away from you. I don't want to wait till tomorrow night. I need to know now." He took her face in his hands. "Will you marry me?"

Carina felt wrapped in a silken cocoon of euphoria. A cry of happiness sprang from her lips. "Yes. I want to be your wife more than anything."

His kiss was slow, thoughtful. "I am one blessed man."

"Well, there's always room in the world for one more blessed man." They pulled apart as Rick walked into the kitchen a crooked grin on his face. "So why are you pestering our houseguest?"

"Your houseguest just agreed to become my wife." Carina almost cried at the pride and happiness in Juan Antonio's voice.

"Oh, girl. You answered too soon. We haven't clued you in on several things. For example, did you know he's a muller?" Rick sat on a bar stool, hooking his legs around the sides. "Yep, he's a muller. He mulls over every decision weeks and weeks at a time. Why, I bet he's wanted to pop the question for months."

"I love that about him." Carina leaned back against Juan Antonio's strong chest. His arms closed around her waist, hands clasping in front.

"And let me tell you about the time…"

"Rick Garret, behave yourself." Marsha walked to her husband who took her into his arms with a huge laugh. "You know Juan Antonio is the catch of the century." Then in a low voice deliberately meant to include Juan Antonio and Carina, she muttered. "What are you doing? Ruining our only hope of getting rid of this guy?"

"Ha, ha, ha. The two of you are so funny." Juan Antonio turned her face sideways to accommodate him as he placed his face against hers. "Not even your teasing can ruin my happiness today. I'm marrying the prettiest woman in Mexico." He kissed her ear. He glanced up at Rick. "You will be my best man, right?"

"Of course. I would be honored." For all his teasing, Rick's voice sounded a little gruff. "What about your brothers?"

"Marcelo and Raul can be ushers."

Carina wondered briefly what Juan Antonio's brothers were like.

"Did you finish the snack bags?" Marsha began to box the ones lying on the table.

"Yes, and there should be several left over, but I'd rather have more than enough rather than too few."

"Right. Me, too." Marsha seemed preoccupied for a moment then asked Rick to take her to the church. She needed to be early for some reason or another. "Carina, will you bring April and the boys when you come? I want Rick to help me with a few things. Rick and I will take the truck and y'all can come in the van."

"Sure thing. Not a problem."

Carina impatiently waited for them to leave then found herself in Juan Antonio's arms again. She giggled like a teenager, realizing they'd been on the same wavelength.

"How soon can you marry me, Ms. Garza?" He nibbled at the edge of her lips. "Do you have to give work a notice or can you just quit on the spot?"

Lost in a world of love and wedding dreams, Carina responded a bit slower than normal.

"Quit what? What notice?" She wished he wouldn't talk so much.

"Your job. How does that work?"

"I don't have to quit my job to get married. I'll simply take a leave of absence for a few weeks before to plan and organize the wedding and a few weeks after for the honeymoon and to move in with you." She reached to kiss his jaw but he pulled away slightly.

"My wife won't need to work. I can provide well for my family."

Carina laughed softly. "I'm so glad to know that, and when the time is right, I'll quit. Until then I'll keep working and saving toward our future."

He took her arms and pulled them from around his neck. "I don't think you understand. I don't want my wife to work. Not even for one day after we're married."

"But that's ridiculous. I love my job. Until we have children what hinders me from working?"

"What hinders you is the fact I don't want a career wife." His voice had taken on an edge reminiscent of the first day she'd met him.

"But you want to marry me, right?" Carina could hear the pleading in her voice but she didn't care. "And I have a career." She reached for his hand and he linked his fingers with hers as if he couldn't help himself.

"Yes, I want to marry you, but it seems the very thing I want from you, you're not willing to give."

Carina stared into his beautiful dark eyes and chose her words well. "Are you really saying that marrying you is conditional on whether or not I quit my job?" She felt ice spreading through her stomach followed by an acute sense of loss.

"For reasons I can't go into right now, yes, that's what I'm saying." His jet-black eyes compelled her to understand.

"Can't or won't?" She was assailed by a terrible sense of bitterness. Mexican macho. She'd lived with this attitude all her life. Her father had ruled her mother's life, never allowing her to make decisions, much less work outside the home.

"Either way, it can't happen." She could hear the defeat in his voice.

"Juan Antonio, I love you. Don't throw what we have away. You're tearing my heart out."

"And I love you, Carina. But shouldn't love be a series of compromises?"

Carina knew all about compromises. "Yes, but compromises are usually one-sided."

"Exactly. If we can't get the first few compromises right, it doesn't bode well for our marriage down the road."

She touched the side of his face lovingly, then moved closer trying to bridge the gap between them. "Love like ours overcomes a lot of obstacles. Let's give it a chance and see where it takes us."

April rushed into the kitchen, unaware that she'd interrupted a serious conversation. The boys followed. "Let's go. We're going to be late." She rushed the kids out the door. Carina leaned in for a kiss and seemingly against his will, Juan Antonio obliged.

All through the evening, Juan Antonio entered and exited her VBS classroom, the laugher and happiness of the previous night sadly absent from his countenance.

When they arrived back at the Garrets', Marsha, ever sensitive to those around her put the kids to bed and retired to her room with Rick. Lights were left on in each room and Carina knew she was being chaperoned and could be walked in on any moment. She was happy and satisfied with this arrangement. She'd made a commitment to the Lord years ago to be pure the day she walked the aisle. She meant to stick to it.

Right now, though, she needed to repair the damage to her relationship with the man she loved. That was the most important thing. She'd tasted love, the real thing. She would not let it slip through her fingers. If last week's experience had taught her anything it was to cherish those loved ones and never take life for granted. It could be snatched from you at a moment's notice.

She turned to find his eyes on her and she walked to him and wrapped her arms around his back. When he enclosed her in a tight embrace she exhaled a huge sigh of relief. Love was a powerful thing.

She drew back to accept the kiss she knew would follow. She was wrong. Instead he withdrew, propped his hips against the kitchen table and crossed his arms.

"I thought…" she stammered.

"Carina, I have a real opposition to my wife working outside the home. It's not some devious plan to control you or rule over you. It's from years of experience. Can you not work with me? This is very, very important to me." His body language pleaded with her to understand. She felt a wretchedness of mind she'd never known before. They were at an impasse.

He saw her answer and she'd not spoken a word. "So you love your job more than me." A glazed look of despair began to spread over his face.

Tears rolled freely down Carina's face. "Never in a million years could I love my job more than you. It's the principle of what you're asking of me."

He pulled her into his arms and gently rocked back and forth as she cried. When he kissed her she tasted his own tears on her lips, then he walked from the kitchen and quietly closed the door. She collapsed onto the floor, deep agonizing sobs racked her body till Marsha gathered her close murmuring dear words of comfort.

Carina finished the next two weeks of work in a fog then packed her bags arriving in Texas the day before her twenty-third birthday. She told no one she was back in town. She simply couldn't face anyone at the moment.

Juan Antonio had flown back to the hacienda the night he left Carina. He'd not answered any of her calls. She got the message. Carina asked her employers to put her on at the Raymondville checkpoint. She filed reports and randomly inspected fruit arriving into and out of the Rio Grande Valley. She moved out of her mother's home into an apartment, to be closer to work. Two months after her brief engagement and breakup she was still walking through life like a zombie. Who knew love could also destroy? Marsha had told her to take one day at a time, and that's what she was doing. The pain had not lessened, but life had gone on and one day she'd be able to understand. Right now she appreciated the days when work took her mind off her heart, but oft as not she dragged home from work and grieved as if someone had died.

Chapter 16

Carina stared out the window at the cars lined up, waiting to pass through the customs inspection. Why had she ever thought less work would help mend her broken heart? She should have asked for the most difficult department at the USDA; then she'd have been too busy to think, much less meditate on things she had no control over. Not that the twenty-mile checkpoint job in Raymondville, Texas, was a piece of cake.

She watched one of the Border Patrol agents motion a van to the side of the road. Something suspicious about the driver or the vehicle must have tipped the agent off. Random searches were not on this week's schedule. Every day, fifty or sixty illegals were deported back to Mexico from Raymondville alone. It never ceased to amaze her just how many repeat offenders there were. They took a chance that one day they would make it through a checkpoint and obtain jobs in the United States.

A tall black-haired guy stepped from the car and Carina gasped. Then the man turned and she saw it was not Juan Antonio. She placed a hand on her heart and took several quick breaths. She clinched her jaw to kill the sob in her throat. Would the pain ever go away? Since Juan Antonio's rejection, she'd waded through a haze of emotions. At first she'd dealt with a boatload of anger, but most of her anger had evaporated, leaving behind mind boggling confusion. One moment, she longed to see him, to tell him she loved him, next she never wanted to see him again. Uppermost in her thoughts was the hope that he was hurting as much as she was. But she wanted him to want her at the same time. What was wrong with her? What had happened to the level-headed young woman who had flown to Mexico just six short months ago?

"Sis, you have a situation outside. Better hustle."

Her brother, Jesse, had been at the station all morning, carefully observing the proceedings of his own Border Patrol Unit. He had been promoted to GL-11 status and now served as senior official over the Raymondville and Falfurius checkpoints. She loved seeing more of him and knew he worried about her. She hadn't felt strong enough to share her burdens with him yet, but he knew she suffered from a broken heart.

She jogged down the outside steps, thankful for the breeze that brushed gently across her face. Yesterday had been hot and dry, the air barely stirring. It seemed unusually hot for November but weather in Texas always proved unpredictable. Next week it could be ten degrees cooler. One never knew.

She stared at the four transfer trucks in surprise. She had two junior agents who did the inspections and she did the paperwork. They had not been in the office all morning and now she saw why. Walking to the back of the first truck she saw boxed grapefruits, which meant this fruit had already gone through a Valley inspection.

"What's the problem, Sal?"

Her newest employee fluttered nervous hands in the air. "We received a report from RGV that the Valley has been quarantined. Fruit fly infestation. These trucks are from the RGV, so we have to inspect each carton of fruit."

Carina heaved a sigh. "*Aye*, this will take the rest of the day so let's get to it. I'll take this one, you take the second truck and tell Chuyito to get the third. We'll all work on the fourth."

Carina dreaded the next few hours in the heat, but the job would require intense concentration which meant her mind could not wander. So for a small while the raw and primitive grief that consumed her life would be forced to take a backseat to her job. She'd learned that hard work helped camouflage the deep despair of loneliness. It didn't dissolve it but it helped. If she focused solely on the grapefruit, Juan Antonio's face would not invade her thoughts. At least not as often.

She waited as Chuyito expertly unloaded the cartons of fruit with the forklift. She opened her first box, taking care not to destroy the cardboard. She knew to repackage would cost the owner more time, wages and money. The driver appeared beside her demanding answers and he was not happy. This was turning into a difficult day.

"Sir, we have to inspect your load. The Rio Grande

Valley has just been quarantined due to a Mexican fruit fly infestation. Your fruit may be perfect but we have to make sure. It's the Texas Department of Agriculture governmental regulations. Now please step aside and allow us to do our job. We will get through a lot faster."

"This is ridiculous. Our orchard is not in the Valley, it's along the outskirts. And we've had no inspection so it can't be our fruit that's infected."

"We will determine that, sir, and then you'll be on your way."

Two hours later, Carina stretched the kinks from her back and looked behind her to see if Chuyito and Sal had finished, as well. To her dismay, four more trucks had joined the line for inspection and if she was not mistaken a very ticked-off, irate owner marched toward her with purposeful intent.

"Who's in charge here?" His tone was offensive but Carina let it ride hoping his aggravation was due to his produce possibly being returned, causing him major financial loss. The cowboy hat he wore must have set him back a pretty penny and then she glanced at his boots. Tres Outlaws, pure ostrich. Expensive taste. She examined his face carefully and realized he was too young to be the owner—must be the son.

"I am, sir." She extended her right hand. To her amazement and apparently against his better judgment he briefly squeezed her hand. So, the young man had good manners. Just maybe he would be reasonable. "How can I help you?"

"These trucks…"

Carina interrupted him, hoping to forgo a long list of complaints. "I need to collect the information from my coworkers and I will let you know the outcome of the inspection on your cargo. If they have nothing to report, you should be on your way shortly."

"These are not from my orchard." He swept his hand to indicate the current work area. "Mine are the four trucks behind this load and my fruit cannot sit in the hot sun for three or four more hours. By the time it gets to market it will have rotted."

Carina glanced at her watch, dreading what she had to tell this man. "Mr...?" She waited for him to supply his name.

"Raul Fuentes."

Carina stood there, blank, amazed and very shaken.

"What? Now that you know my name you're going to hit me with a fine, right?" The man placed his hands on his hips, a fierce look entering his eyes.

"Of course not. Your name... I once loved someone with that last name." Carina's body stiffened in shock. Had she said the words out loud?

She glanced up and saw a gleam of interest enter the man's eyes but all he said was, "Yeah, we Fuentes men are a lovable lot, so be a love, okay, and get our fruit on the road."

Carina excused herself and hurried to the office. Her face felt sunburned, but she hadn't been in the sun. Chuyito came in behind her and they discussed the fruit they had inspected. Sal came in midway through their reporting and began the same process. They worked together for about an hour, cataloging the number of cartons, making certain of the address and owner's name, placing dates and times, then Carina filled out reports, signed them and stamped a copy for the driver. She glanced at the clock and it was six fifty-five. The other trucks would have to wait till morning. She must break the news to another Fuentes that she could not help him, could not be a "love" and get his fruit on the road.

She walked outside to find him on his cell phone, pacing back and forth, gesturing wildly as he explained the delay.

"So, what's the verdict, ma'am?"

"Mr. Fuentes, we'll start on your load first thing in the morning."

"What? No, no, my fruit cannot sit here overnight in this heat. Isn't there someone that will do the inspections? I will gladly pay your overtime."

"Sir, there is nothing more to be done. It will not damage the fruit. Leave your doors open and the breeze will pass through. Besides, the sun's going down and the natural light will be gone about an hour after it sets."

"But you have floodlights."

"With this type of inspection, we rely on natural light because the fruit flies will hide from the electric lights. I'm sorry. It cannot be helped." Carina sought just the right inflection of voice to hopefully alleviate the man's anger.

"Well, this will not do. Who's your boss? I need someone to get my load through now."

"I am the agent in charge here. We've already stayed two hours over to complete the man's load ahead of you. You may pull your trucks under the awning if you think that will help." Carina's voice brooked no argument and she felt she'd given the man enough of her attention. She turned to walk away and heard the man speak in Spanish to the occupant on the other end of his cell phone. "There is a woman in charge here and she doesn't think this is important."

Without considering her actions, Carina turned and

addressed the man in Spanish. "This woman does think
this is important. That's why she isn't willing to permit bad fruit to make it to market and make some child
sick."

She entered her office, grabbed her purse and headed
out the back way to her car. She'd had enough for one
day. She wanted a hot bath, a cold shower and a good
book. Her body was so tired. She knew emotional drain
caused most of her fatigue, but she felt at a loss as to
what to do. How did you make heartache disappear?

Forty-five minutes later she pulled into a parking
spot in front of her apartment. She didn't remember
the drive home, only the conflicting emotions that had
become her constant companions. She had thought she
could do without Juan Antonio in her life but she'd
begun to wonder if she shouldn't have accepted his
conditions and quit her job. At least that way she would
still have him in her life instead of this big, gaping hole.

At times, she could still feel the touch of his hand
as he brushed the hair off her forehead; the strength
of his arms as he folded them around her. She'd given
all that up for a principle, but principles didn't stave
off loneliness, nor take your hand during a plane ride.
He'd placed restrictions on her, but wasn't marriage a
fifty-fifty partnership? Sooner or later she might have
required something of him.

Lately she'd hated getting out of bed and reporting
to work. Most days, it was all she could do to put one
foot in front of the other, and she would have loved
being a stay-at-home wife. She knew that in her heart.
It had always been her plan to stop working when she
had kids, so why had she cut her nose off to spite her
face? *Because of you, Dad. I gave up the man of my*

*dreams because I didn't want to live my life married to
a man who took away my right to make my own decisions. Like you did with Mom.*

Carina stepped into the shower, letting the hot water
dissolve the sweaty grapefruit stickiness from her tired
body. From now till a few weeks after Christmas they'd
be overrun with citrus cargo and with the added aggravation of the fruit fly their workload would double. Normally she loved her work, and to think she protected the
people of the U.S. gave her pure satisfaction. But her
life had lost its purpose. *Lord, when will I get over this?*

She entered the kitchen clad in pajama pants and
T-shirt and quickly made herself an egg and bacon taquito. Un-emptied boxes sat on the countertops and
floor. She'd moved in three days after returning to the
States. She had needed to be alone; to grieve and nurse
her wounds in private. But other than the necessities,
everything was still boxed up.

She remembered sharing the same meal with Juan
Antonio and how he'd wiped the plate with the last
bite of his tortilla. Her appetite left and she laid the
food back on her plate. Tears began a steady trickle
down her cheeks and she hurried to the living room
and grabbed her Bible.

In the past two months, the grand old Book had been
the only thing that eased the pain in her heart. It fell
open at a well-worn passage and she read the words
slowly, letting them minister to her soul. *Psalms 73:26
My flesh and my heart faileth, but God is the strength
of my heart, and my portion forever.* Then she turned to
what had become her favorite. *Psalm 147:3 He heals the
broken-hearted and binds up their wounds.* She bowed
her head to pray and only moans proceeded from her

mouth. Somehow, though, she felt God understood everything she could not say and the cry heavy upon her heart was *Lord, please, bring him back to me.*

How long she sat and stared into space she didn't know but the doorbell interrupted and she went to answer it, walking like a sixty-year-old grandma.

"Mom! What are you doing here? Come in." Carina knew she looked a mess but for once she didn't care. Her mother would love her no matter what. She fought back tears wishing Juan Antonio had loved her that much.

"Carina, I've been so worried about you." Her mother's pronunciation of her name reminded her of the way Juan Antonio said it. "Ka-deen-nah." "Jesse told me you'd lost weight and that you weren't doing your job. What's wrong, *mi hija?*"

Oh, thanks a lot, big brother. Carina wondered what else Jesse had told their mom.

"I do my job, Mother. Jesse exaggerated. You know he always does." She motioned her mom to the sofa.

"Well, he didn't exaggerate about the weight loss. *Estas muy flaca. Por que?*"

"I'm not skinny. Maybe working in the fields in Mexico took a little weight off. I don't know." Memories flooded her mind and Carina stifled a sob, but when her mother opened her arms she fell into them crying, compulsive sobs that shook her body. She wept aloud as her mother gently rocked her back and forth. Sorrow weighed upon her until her sense of loss went beyond tears. She pulled her legs up on the sofa and laid her head in her mother's lap. While her mother smoothed the hair off her brow she explained her loss in jagged, broken sentences interspersed with hiccups and fits of tears.

When she told her mother about Juan Antonio's ultimatum her mother's muttered *"Macho"* was her only comment.

"Mi amor, why did you find this demand so *dificil?* You always wanted to stay home with the *niños,* no?"

"Yes, Mother, but don't you see? Our marriage would be just like yours and *Papi*'s. He made all the decisions and you never had a voice. I want a partnership for a marriage. I want my opinions and desires to count. Is that too much to ask?"

Her mother lifted Carina's head from her lap, forcing her to sit up. She took Carina's face between her hands. *"Mi hija,* where on this earth did you get such a...a...*loca* idea?"

"What do you mean?" Carina drew back and looked intently at her mother. She had no desire to hurt her feelings but she needed her mother to understand. "I watched him do it time after time. You never spoke up for yourself. Not once did he even allow you to choose the paint colors for the house, even the kitchen though he never ever worked in that room."

"Carina, listen to me and listen well. When your father and I married, there were so many decisions to be made concerning his citizenship in this country." Her mother shrugged matter-of-factly. "It was all, how you say, *sobre mi cabeza,* over my head, but he felt more secure here at the border so we moved here. I wanted to be with him. I loved him *con total mi vida.* I wanted his babies and him. Nothing else mattered to me." She spread her hands in appeal. "I hated making decisions, so it was wonderful to have him make them for me. But he never—listen to me, *hija*—never once made a major decision without consulting me. Sometimes we argued over what to do, so he would wait until we agreed before he ever chose for us."

Carina remained motionless for a moment in denial at her mother's simple explanation. "I never heard him ask you for your opinion. Not once, and I never saw you argue with him." Carina heard the disbelief in her voice and hoped her mom would not be offended.

"Your dad was like your Juan Antonio, *hija. Macho Mejicana!* To argue with *Papi* in public would have dishonored him. He thought it would teach you *ninos* to disrespect him, so we agreed we would never argue in front of you and we didn't. That stayed behind our bedroom doors. I loved that he took care of me so well. He was a man, not an *endeble.*"

"No," Carina said thoughtfully, "he definitely wasn't a wimp." A different kind of sorrow tore at Carina's already ravaged heart. She'd had unkind thoughts toward her dad most of her adult life, starting in high school. She'd wanted to take home economics and he'd not allowed it. A new thought struck her.

"Mom, if you and *Papi* reached all major decisions together, why didn't you stand up for me when I wanted to take home economics in the ninth grade?"

"Your dad actually took your side on that one, *amor,* but I said no."

"But why?"

"Because, my beautiful daughter, *I* wanted to teach you to cook and to sew and to clean house. I wanted you to learn from *su madre,* the same way I learned."

For the first time in months, Carina felt a smile tip the corners of her mouth. "We had such fun, didn't we, *Mami?*" To say her mother's explanation had been a revelation was putting it mildly, and the strain from her breakup with Juan Antonio seemed to lessen in the nostalgic moments shared with her precious mother.

"We surely did, *hija.* I will treasure those times for the rest of *mi vida.*" She intertwined her fingers with Carina's and shifted sideways to pull Carina back into her arms. "Now I want to tell you something very important."

Carina relaxed against her mother's side, her mind and body slowly finding peace.

"Men are funny creatures, *hija.*"

"Tell me about it," Carina interrupted.

"No, *hija,* you will listen, not talk, so that I can help you, because I cannot stand to see your heart so broken."

"Sorry, *Mami.*"

If she ever got the chance to be a mother, she hoped she'd be just like her own, because her mother had poured salve over her wounded heart tonight. What a treasure she had.

"Most men appear to be confident, strong and determined, but many times they need to be certain of our love. Sometimes they test a woman, issue ultimatums like your Juan Antonio did. Most of the time, it is a cry for reassurance. A woman can break or make a man. If she has too much control, he becomes weak and they both are dissatisfied. If he rules with a rod of iron, she is dissatisfied. A man does not think like a woman so he is not going to think about things like this. He just takes each day as it comes, does his best for the woman he loves. So let me ask you a question. Did you say no to his proposal because you wanted to make him bow to your will?"

"No, Mom! Nothing like that." Carina sat up, indignation stiffening her spine. "That's what he did to me."

"And you retaliated in like manner." When Carina started to protest, her mother lifted her hand to silence her. "*Sí, mi hija, exactamento.* It is the same. You both needed to trust, but you didn't. Tell me, do you think the outcome would have been different if you had said, 'Okay, *mi amor,* I love you with every fiber of my being and if that is what you need me to do, then consider it done. Because you are the most important person to me and I love you more than life itself.'

A new anguish seared her heart. If she hadn't been so hasty, so stubborn, she could have been planning her wedding to the man she loved exactly as her mother stated.

"Oh, *Mami,* what do I do?"

"You find this man, and you tell him how you feel."

The wheels were already turning in Carina's mind. What if Juan Antonio had sold the plantation? Where had he moved to?

She followed her mother to the door experiencing a gamut of perplexing emotions.

"And *hija,* may I give you a word of warning?"

"Yes?"

Carina's mother kissed her on the cheek and gave a brief hug before she continued speaking. "Always weigh your words before you speak. You are, after all, natured like your *Papi.* That's why you're so special to me."

Her mother's chuckle wrapped around her, causing a warm glow to flow through her. She had a lot of thinking to do, decisions to make, but Carina felt hope. Hugging it close to her chest she locked the door, cutting the lights as she headed for the bedroom. She needed sleep and tonight there were no shadows across her heart.

Chapter 17

"Morning, boss."

Carina lifted one hand in greeting then dropped into her office chair. "So…seven trucks waiting. Guess we have our work cut out for us today."

"Yep, and the owner from yesterday is already here this morning." Sal delivered the news matter-of-factly. "It's the Citrus Queen Orchard."

"But it's only six o'clock. Why's he here so early?" Carina had plans to do internet searches for one Juan Antonio Fuentes while waiting for the guys to inspect the first of the cargo. It wasn't unusual for them to start the process and she'd join them later when most of the paperwork had been done.

"No idea. There's actually nothing he can do to help lift the quarantine, but if he feels better being here I've got no problem with it." Chuyito knew the routine better than Carina, but he never usurped her authority and they had a healthy respect for each other as colleagues. Sal, on the other hand, couldn't wait to become an office agent, making decisions from the comfort of a cushy chair.

Carina gave each man a schedule for the day. Sal pulled the first few hours working with the oncoming traffic and Chuy started inspection on the waiting trucks.

"Let's not hold up any of the trucks carrying vegetables. We'll do standard inspects, and Sal, call me immediately if traffic backs up so we can stay ahead if possible."

The two men left her office already deep in conversation about fajitas and rice for lunch. She watched till they disappeared around the corner then hurriedly typed in Juan Antonio's name. As she waited on the slow connection to the internet she watched a helicopter swoop from the sky and disappear behind the building. Border Patrol must be bringing in some top dogs. Jesse hadn't said he expected anyone. They worked in opposite ends of the old building that housed both the agriculture division of the USDA and the Border Patrol. They had been promised a new building but so far that's all it had been. A promise.

"Who's in charge here?"

Carina heard the voice full of irritation, questioning Chuy as he opened the door to the outer office.

"I'll take you to her, sir." The respect in Chuy's voice alerted Carina that one of the "top dogs" she'd thought belonged to the Border Patrol must actually belong to her unit. She quickly exited the search engine and stood to greet whoever it was. Then she merely stared, tongue-tied. Juan Antonio. She heard his quick intake of breath.

His eyes searched her face, as if probing her very thoughts. His eyebrows rose enquiringly and there was a suspicious line at the corners of his mouth. Could it be that he'd gone through his own private hell over their separation? She longed to run to him, to sift her fingers through his dark hair and pull his face down for a kiss. Her legs began to tremble and she felt for the chair behind her.

"Carina?" His impersonal tone broke the stillness.

"Juan Antonio, what are you doing here?" She could hardly lift her voice above a whisper. She wanted to tell him she was sorry. That she had changed her mind. How would he react if she simply said what was in her heart?

"My brother's trucks are lined up outside and we have five more on the way. This is his biggest harvest in eight years. He lost most of his trees in the freeze in '08 and, as you know, it takes several years to repair the damage to the grove." He ran a hand through his hair then smoothed it back down. She saw his jaw tense, a sure sign of frustration. "He's up to his eyeballs in payments to the bank, but this harvest will see him back on his feet." He looked at her intently, a spark of some indefinable emotion in his black eyes. "Can you help?"

That God had placed this situation right into her lap she had no doubt. Hadn't she begged him for another chance to prove her love to this proud man? She would not miss this chance.

"We will have your trucks on the road as soon as humanly possible. Let me make a few calls, and I'll start the inspection myself."

His smile brought an immediate softening to his features. He turned toward the door but paused, his back to her. He spun back around and his mouth twisted wryly. "How are you, Carina?"

Carina tried to keep all emotion from her voice. Her thoughts scrambled, her heart aching.

"I'm good, Tonio. You?" Without being aware, she'd called him by her pet name for him.

"I've been better." His voice sounded tired.

"Did you sell the plantation?"

"Yes, a couple of weeks after you left, a buyer came through, but it took six weeks to complete the sale. Lots of red tape in Mexico."

He made it sound as if she chose to leave. From some inner strength she straightened herself with dignity. He had driven her away. She was suddenly overwhelmed by the torment of the past few weeks. All resolve to make things right fled out the window, replaced by accusations and pain. She wanted to lash out, to pierce his cool, aloof manner just once. She resisted with every means in her power.

"I'm glad you got things settled."

They stared at each other across a sudden uneasy silence. She remained absolutely motionless, half in anticipation, half in dread. If he truly loved her, how could he have endured the pain of their separation? Why had he not come after her? Maybe she should just accept the fact that it was over and move on.

Then she remembered the endless nights of crying, the cold despair that had been her constant companion. This man completed her. Without him, she wasn't whole. Surely a love like that was worth fighting for.

"I'd better get started on your trucks. Time is our enemy today."

He inclined his head in a polite nod, muttered a brief thanks and was gone.

For some time after he left, Carina sat perfectly still, her mind a jumble of myriad emotions. If she had expected an immediate capitulation on either of their parts to end this battle of wills, she'd certainly been disappointed. She settled back, searching for direction. *Lord, what do I do now?* A verse suddenly came into her mind. *Love suffers long and is kind...* She had suffered, and it felt like an eternity. Every time she sought the scriptures, she received hope, a strength that quieted the anguish in her soul. She had no other option but to trust there was still a chance for her to grow whole again.

God brought them together today. This is what she'd prayed for. He had answered prayer. The Lord had provided her a golden opportunity to help Juan Antonio with the very job he had tried to deny her. Powerful relief filled her. The Lord guided her steps and she was on track. With a pulse-pounding certainty she knew what she had to do. She reached for the phone, taking charge with quiet assurance.

"What's the plan?"

Juan Antonio walked to where his younger brother stood, trying to disguise his irritation at Raul's annoying habit of procrastinating. Had he loaded the grapefruit two days earlier as scheduled, they could have avoided all this hassle. But no, Raul's motto was never do today what you can put off till tomorrow. *Mañana*—his favorite word.

"Carina's on it. She'll let us know something in a bit."

"You're already on a first-name basis with the female

agent. Good work, bro." Raul raised his hand for a fist bump, but Juan Antonio was not amused.

"Cut it out, Raul. I shouldn't have to remind you how serious this is." Juan Antonio could hear the critical tone in his voice but he'd about reached the end of his rope. He'd arrived home from Mexico to find his two brothers at odds with each other and he'd been forced to play peacemaker. Both were great guys but Marcelo had little patience for Raul's laid-back lifestyle. The three of them had inherited their maternal grandfather's land; five thousand acres of prime ranch land except for the two-hundred-acre orchard known to the Rio Grande Valley as the Citrus Queen.

"Sorry, J.T., didn't mean to offend."

At Juan Antonio's birth, Marcelo, who'd been eighteen months at the time, hadn't been able to say the long name and he'd tried for the shorter version of Juan Tonio. That had been impossible, too, so *Papi* shortened it to J.T. Then four years later Raul came along and, until high school, had called him by the initials. Raul's slip into the boyhood name reminded Juan Antonio that his twenty-two-year-old brother had taken on a heavy load; a load that an older man would have found daunting to say the least.

Marcelo, the oldest of the brothers, had chosen the western parcel of land, which actually lay in a different county, just north of Edinburg. He'd developed it into successful cattle-raising property. He ran over fifteen hundred head of prime Hereford cattle; had built a home and moved away from the Citrus Queen homestead.

Raul had inherited their father's green thumb and had chosen the orchards and the old home place. He'd gone to college at Texas A&M and obtained a business degree, but at times the overhead of the business and the upkeep on the house overwhelmed him, and deadlines zoomed past with no more importance than a pesky mosquito. Marcelo and Juan Antonio finally hired a manager and things had gone much smoother, but the woman could only do so much.

Juan Antonio planned to raise sugarcane in the eastern section of land. The sale of the mango plantation in Mexico had set him up. He had the plans for a Spanish hacienda and the foundations were ready to be poured. That the joy those plans usually brought had lessened was not lost on him. For too long now, his whole body had been engulfed in tides of weariness and despair. He felt drained, hollow, lifeless. The exact same thing that caused his dad's early death had happened to him. The woman he loved had chosen her career over him. Memories ate at a man's gut and left him in a wasteland of want.

All three sections of the Fuentes brothers' inheritance had to show a profit for them to succeed, which was why he'd flown here today to correct another of Raul's mistakes. He dared not think Carina's presence anything other than a coincidence, because to think otherwise would bring hope, and he dealt only in reality these days.

"Juan Antonio?" He turned and headed toward Carina as soon as he heard her voice. Like a moth to the flame, he still felt powerless to resist being close to her.

"What's up?" Tiny curling tendrils escaped the clasp holding the honey-silken mass of hair and his fingers ached to smooth it behind her ear.

"I've managed to secure three more agents...they'll

be here in about thirty minutes. With three per truck, we should get all your trucks out by the end of the day."

"Can't you just do one or two and ascertain that they're all bug-free?"

She looked up from her notes and squinted at him through the sun shining in her eyes. "Not since your trucks arrived the evening after they issued the quarantine." She shifted from foot to foot and the shock of discovery hit Juan Antonio full force. Carina was nervous. Not even when they faced Don Diego had she been nervous. She always had an air of calm and self-confidence that he loved. He stepped in front of her to block the sun. "If I could pass them, I would, Tonio. It's not like I'm doing this on purpose. I promise."

"I know, Carina. I just want to get it over with. What do you need me to do?" He made a slight gesture with his right hand and they turned toward the trucks.

"Nothing. The best thing you can do is stay out of the way. We'll get done a lot quicker."

"Can I use your office? I have some paperwork to do."

She rounded the back of the truck just as the forklift moved the first load sideways. Without thinking his arm encircled her waist and he pulled her back against him out of harm's way. "Careful." His instinctive response to her was so powerful. He loved her with every beat of his heart. She was his woman. The only one for him. Why wasn't that enough for her? He withdrew his arm, his movements awkward and stiff. This was torture. He turned on his heel and strode to the office door.

Marcelo and Raul already occupied the outer break room area. He hurried past them to the privacy of Carina's office. He'd just managed to lean back in her chair when the doorway filled with both brothers. Raul had called yesterday about the delay, so Marcelo had flown them over in his helicopter, lovingly tagged the "cattle-copter," since they used it to spot stray cattle after storms. Both brothers now stared at him intently; Marcelo with eyes narrowed and Raul sporting a silly grin on his face. Juan Antonio allowed a silken thread of warning to enter his voice.

"What's up?"

"Why don't you tell us, little brother, what's going on between you and Ms. Fruit Inspector." Marcelo's mellow baritone sounded controlled, as if he wasn't above wrestling Juan Antonio to the floor and pummeling it out of him. His words seemed to amuse Raul even more.

"Not that it's any of your business, *big brother,* but there's nothing going on."

"Mmm-hmm. So that's why you can't keep your hands off her."

Juan Antonio jumped to his feet, anger radiating through every pore. "Watch your mouth, Marcelo."

Marcelo lifted both hands in appeal. "Take it easy, J.T. I meant no disrespect."

The defensiveness went right out of him. What was he doing, picking a fight with his brothers? At least they loved him. He sat down and ran trembling hands through his hair. When he looked up Marcelo and Juan sat across from him, in front of the desk. He couldn't control his burst of laughter. They looked like two vultures circling for the kill. "Two old women."

"The difference, little brother, between us and 'two old women' is that they would gossip to others about what you're getting ready to share with us. We—" Marcelo pointed first to himself then to Raul "—have no desire to spread it, just help a brother in his misery. Now what gives?"

"You want the short version or the long?"

"Short."

"Short."

Both men answered simultaneously. Juan Antonio had already decided on saying the least possible to get them off his back. If he didn't tell them something they'd follow him and watch everything he did, examining each little detail till they drove him mad or he spilled the beans. In the short time they'd seen him with Carina they'd created a corkscrewed scenario to fit their own ideas.

"We met at *Abuelo's* in *Mejico*. She was the NAFTA inspector. I thought there might be a future for us but I was wrong. End of story." Juan Antonio kept his voice matter-of-fact to stave off any questions. He should have known it wouldn't work.

"There are a lot of holes in your story, J.T." Raul glanced uneasily at Marcelo for support. In most all the family discussions, Raul wound up on the receiving end of the conversation, usually on the defensive. It wasn't often he questioned one of his older brothers. Judging by his silent appeal for help from Marcelo, it made him uncomfortable. Juan Antonio wondered why he'd never noticed it before. How long had it been since the three of them had been camping together, or fishing? When had it gotten to the place they couldn't speak freely with each other? A sudden twinge of guilt added to his feeling of emptiness. He'd let his brothers down, too. When had his life become so joyless, so disappointing?

"There are no holes. That's it in a nutshell."

"Shot you down, didn't she? Ouch, that hurts."

"No, Raul, she did not. I actually ended it." Juan Antonio swallowed the familiar suffocating anguish that threatened to close his throat.

"But why?" Raul spread his hands questioningly. "She's a babe!"

"And if she liked your ugly mug what could have been the problem?" Marcelo sat forward and looked at him intently.

"She loved her career more."

Marcelo shrugged his shoulders and leaned back. "So she was actually the one that said no."

Juan Antonio pushed to his feet and began to pace the small area behind the desk. He caught a quick glimpse of Carina before she disappeared around a truck.

"No, she said yes. I said no." At the confused look on his brothers' faces, Juan Antonio returned to the chair and spread his hands on the desk. "I asked her to marry me. She said yes. I asked her to quit her job. She said no. It ended almost before it began." *Except for the glorious hours you spent getting to know each other,* his heart said in a broken whisper.

"Well, there you go. No one wants a wife who won't obey. Kick 'em to the curb. That's what I tell Adele will happen to her one day if she keeps shooting off her mouth." Raul nodded his head as if agreeing with himself.

"Raul, if you cause Adele to quit, I will take it out of your hide. She's the best office manager slash housekeeper you've ever had." Marcelo issued the warning as if dealing with a temperamental child. His expressive face changed and became almost somber when he looked back at Juan Antonio. "Let me get this straight.

You issued an ultimatum. Either you or the job?" He tilted his brow questioningly.

"Right."

"Did you go completely daft? Why, for pity's sake?" Marcelo's expression was one of pained tolerance. Much like when they were kids it made Juan Antonio defensive.

"Have you forgotten what Mother's career did to our family? The crying, the separation and heartbreak? I didn't want that for me or for my children."

"Well," Raul reasoned, "women these days have learned how to have a home and a career. It wouldn't necessarily be like that."

"J.T., as usual, you got it all wrong. It wasn't Mom's career that kept us separated. It was *Papi*'s mule-headed stubbornness over those cursed mangoes. Mother's career paid the workers and the upkeep on that monstrosity you just sold." Marcelo smacked a hand on the desk and stood to his feet. "I'd like to stay and continue this little heart-to-heart but I've got my own situation to deal with over at the line shack." He looked questioningly at Juan Antonio. "You going with me or catching a ride with Raul?"

"What do you mean his stubbornness? It was Mother who always brought us back to the States. She had to get back to her job." Juan Antonio had a hard time wrapping his mind around Marcelo's words.

"What's going on at the line shack?" Raul asked.

Marcelo ignored Raul and answered Juan Antonio. "Think about it, J.T. Who did the crying? Mother and us, right? Why would she cry if she was returning to a job she loved? She cried because she didn't want to leave."

"Who cares? That's all water under the bridge. Get over it or get therapy. Now, what happened at the line shack?" Raul's exasperation showed in the heavy sarcasm in his voice.

Marcelo stared at Raul a moment. "Raul, you don't have an ounce of compassion in you. One of these days some girl's going to wipe that smirk off your face and stomp all over your heart. Maybe then you'll grow up."

He walked stiffly to the door, pulling at his jean legs so they fell over the tops of his boots. He placed his hands on the door frame and looked out into the break room for a moment. When he turned back around he had a sheepish grin on his face and his voice was a little awkward. "Makayla Cana's granddaughter finally showed up to claim her inheritance. Problem is, she passed the broken-down old home place she inherited and drove on up the hill to my line shack. She moved in. Lock, stock and barrel."

"Hello." Juan Antonio was too surprised to say more. He shot a quick look at Raul and burst out laughing.

Raul snapped his open mouth shut and shook his head in utter disbelief. "You two bazooka heads have all the luck. Women just fall into your laps and what do you do? You analyze the situation, weigh all the pros and cons and end up losing her." He gave both brothers a black layered look. "Neither of you know how to treat a woman. Why can't these things ever happen to me?" He brushed by Marcelo in the doorway calling back over his shoulder. "I'm going home. They don't need me here babysitting the fruit."

Juan Antonio watched Marcelo's face split into a wide grin. "Remember, J.T., what fun we used to have devising ways to make him mad so he'd run tell Mama, giving us a chance to hide?"

In spite of himself, Juan Antonio chuckled. "Yeah, Marc, I remember, but we've got to stop doing that. He's a grown man and if we don't treat him like one he's going to forever run instead of taking responsibility."

"I guess so." Marcelo bent his head slightly forward, inspecting his boots. "Are you going to be all right?"

Juan Antonio swallowed the unfamiliar insecurity threatening to choke him. "I'll be fine. Thanks."

"You going with me?"

"No, I think I'll hang around here…see if I might help in some way."

Marcelo nodded and walked out the door. Juan Antonio knew they both had an aversion to goodbyes. Knew it and accepted it. They'd had enough of those as kids to last them a lifetime.

Chapter 18

Carina pushed the damp hair off her forehead and drank the last half of the lemonade Juan Antonio had handed her. At three-twenty in the afternoon, he'd decided he had waited long enough for food. He borrowed her car and drove to a Whataburger restaurant on I-77 for lunch and had ignored her denial of anything to eat or drink. He'd brought her back a Whataburger Jr combo. She'd thanked him graciously, unable to stop the happy smile on her face. Who in their right mind would pass up a Whataburger?

In college she'd talked up the restaurant so much she finally persuaded a friend from North Carolina to join her one night after a ball game. Her friend had called it "What a disappointment." But Carina loved the food. She stopped in the mornings for a sausage biscuit or a breakfast taquito of potato, bacon and egg, and a large sweet tea.

"I thought the saying was, 'a way to a *man's* heart was through his stomach,'" Juan Antonio teased from across the break room table.

She wiped her mouth with a napkin, wrinkled her nose and shook her head. "I'll trade you my heart any day for a Whataburger." Shock flew through her. What had she just said? She looked up.

"I may just take you up on that." He said the words tentatively as if testing the idea.

She felt as if they both were tiptoeing their way around each other. She chose her words carefully.

"My heart already belongs to you, Juan Antonio." Her hands trembled as she pushed her hair behind her ears. She folded them in front of her on the table.

His expression stilled and grew serious. His gaze traveled over her face and searched her eyes. The very air around her seemed electrified; her mind a crazy mixture of hope and fear.

She watched his lids slip down over his beautiful eyes, hiding his thoughts from her. Her mind refused to register the significance of that. He leaned forward, placing his arms on the tabletop, and covered her hands with his. Of their own volition her fingers laced together with his. Carina's whole being seemed to be filled with waiting. His silence gnawed away at her confidence.

She could stand it no longer. "Tonio?" She barely raised her voice above a whisper.

The heavy lashes that shadowed his cheeks flew up. She merely stared, tongue-tied. Unspoken pain was alive and glowing in his eyes. So he, too, had suffered.

The misery of their time apart enveloped them and her eyes filled; one lone tear ran down her cheek.

With a moan of distress he brought her hands to his lips, placing a firm kiss on each one before releasing them. His chair scraped backward and in a frenetic dash he was out the door.

Smothering a sob, Carina fled to her office.

Juan Antonio placed his hands on the hood of a parked car and bent over in pain. One scene after another coruscated through his mind, clarifying youthful misconceptions. So clearly, as if just yesterday he saw and felt the clinging, tearful goodbye to his dad. He remembered sitting on his mother's lap, his head on her shoulder, face buried in her neck as he wept, bereft and desolate. She held him close, her other arm encircling Marcelo as her tears mingled with theirs. They had been too small to suffer such heartbreak.

Later years flashed before him, when he'd refused her offer of comfort, lashing out at her for taking them away from his beloved *Papi*. Never once had she punished him or defended herself even though he'd accused her many times of breaking up their home. Why had she not explained? His mind spun with bewilderment.

Then Carina infringed upon his thoughts, laughing up at him, teasing, and declaring her love. He'd tarred her with the same brush as his mother. She'd fought like a lioness to stay with him, arguing that his feelings about her job had no rhyme or reason. He'd denied her his love, yet just now she'd proclaimed him owner of her heart.

A soft whisper breathed against his ear. *Just like Carina, I still love you. You've held me at arm's length*

*and my heart has grieved. You are my child but I will
not force a fellowship you do not desire.*

"Oh, Lord," Juan Antonio groaned, tears rolling unbidden down his face. "I'm so sorry."

Traffic and voices intruded into his soul-searching
and he had to get out of there, to be alone. He needed
to talk to the Savior before he could go any further. He
was at the end of his rope, and surrendering dangled
blessed relief and hope in front of him. He still had Carina's keys in his pocket. He opened the door of her vehicle and climbed inside. A few moments later he pulled
to the farthest end of a rest area and, holding tightly to
the steering wheel, he laid his head in the crook of his
arm. Huge sobs shook his body and he pressed the back
of his hand over his mouth to stifle the sound.

All the hurt he'd carried since childhood slowly
began to seep from his heart. The fear of loving someone lest they be yanked from his life began to grow
dimmer and he wept bitterly over the little boy who had
held on so tightly and still lost in the end.

He cried over the troubled years with his precious
mother. How he'd needed her in high school and college. He'd longed to sit at the kitchen table as Marcelo
had done, and pour out all his troubles to her, but instead he'd held on to the anger, denying her the chance
to hurt him again.

He'd built such a high wall against Carina, but she'd
crashed through and the pain of losing her had turned
him inside out, ripping him apart. Now he understood;
this fear of loss, of being hurt and his own insecurity
had sabotaged his relationship with her. The pain had
been so great, at times he wanted to hide away from
the world and lick his wounds like a dog.

But the lost relationship that finally brought him to his knees was the one with his Savior. "Lord," His choked voice could only whisper. "Please forgive me. I'm not deserving of Your love and grace but I want them and need You so much. I'm so sorry, Lord, for the bitterness, the accusations and stubbornness. I didn't know what to do or who to trust, but Lord, I knew You were there, waiting and compelling me to come home. Please forgive me, Lord, make me strong. In Jesus's name."

The balm being poured over the anguish in his soul began to soothe his spirit; the ravages left by mistrust, smoothly covered over. He felt as if arms encircled him, gently rocking till all the despair, the fear and the anger left his body.

For the first time in years, he sat in perfect peace and harmony of the soul. He felt too weak to even start the car. Gradually his strength returned and like a homing pigeon he headed straight to the woman he loved.

Carina splashed cold water on her swollen eyes and then patted her face dry. Thankfully no one had entered the restroom, though it probably wouldn't have mattered. She couldn't have controlled the tears any more than she could hold up the clouds. She looked in the mirror at the woman staring back at her. *What do we do now?*

"Carina?"

She recognized Juan Antonio's voice calling her name.

"Carina, where are you?"

She opened the restroom door just as Juan Antonio raised his hand to knock. He clutched her hand, pulling her along behind him down the hall to her office. She was too startled by his actions to offer any resistance. At her office he propelled them both inside and closed the door. She turned to question him only to have his arms encircle her, one hand in the small of her back the other wound in her hair. She felt the tremors in his chest and heard the sob catch in his throat. She wound her arms around his back and buried her face against the corded muscles of his shoulder. The sweetness of his embrace, the brokenness she sensed in him chased away the emptiness and hopelessness she'd experienced when he'd left earlier. They remained like that for long moments.

She felt his mouth against her brow and then he took her head between his hands, turning her face up to his. His kiss touched her like a whisper, lips soft and moist. Loving hands slid down her arms, entwining their fingers. He stepped back, putting space between them.

"Carina, what you said before…about your heart belonging to me. Is that true?"

She searched his face anxiously. He'd spoken no words of love, had made no promises. It appeared she must be the one to commit with complete trust. It didn't matter. Without him, she felt incomplete. There was no other recourse to consider.

"Yes." Her husky voice shook. She cleared her throat and said firmly, "Yes, it's the truth."

He touched his brow to hers. "And mine to you." Softly his breath fanned her face. Carina's heart sang with delight. She gloried in the shared moment, while heartache, loneliness and hopelessness became painful memories in the back recesses of her mind. Memories she hoped never to rekindle.

He gently urged her toward the chairs in front of her

desk and when she was seated he clasped her hands in his. "There are things in my life that I need answers to, that need to be settled before we can move on. They have nothing to do with you except that they are misconceptions that caused me not to trust you and almost destroyed us." A muscle flickered in his jaw and Carina tenderly smoothed a hand along his cheek. He clasped her wrist and gently kissed her palm. He placed her hand against his heart. "I need to go visit my mother. I want you to come with me."

"Will you answer something for me first?" Perhaps it was simply her own insecurity, but old fears caused a niggle of doubt inside Carina. After all he'd walked away from her not more than thirty minutes ago. "Do you love me?" Her voice cracked and she held her breath, holding pure raw emotion in check.

She felt, rather than saw, his shocked movement. "Have you no idea how I feel?" She shook her head. "*Aye,* you don't, do you." He rubbed the back of his neck shaking his head in self-recrimination. Something intense flared in his eyes. "I keep getting it wrong, don't I? I'm sorry, Carina. Come here." He dropped down in front of her chair, his arms encircling her waist, drawing them close together. "My precious, fiery, stubborn sweetheart. I love you with every fiber of my being. Without you—" he made a slight gesture with his right hand "—even breathing hurts."

"I know. Oh, Juan Antonio, I lost my way. Nothing worked." Carina touched his hair, then the side of his face.

"The days ran into one long day or night. I couldn't think...or finish a sentence." He kissed the tip of her nose.

She pressed both hands over her eyes as if they

burned with the weariness and despair she had experienced, but he removed them gently and kissed her closed lids.

"Let's agree together, Carina, right now, to never let this happen to us again. We'll talk things out...argue even, but never leave each other. When you walked away, you gutted me."

That thought should have pleased Carina, but a vivid recollection of her own pain the past few months caused her to commiserate with him. She felt saddened that they had hurt each other and wasted precious time they could have shared together.

"As long as you'll have me, Antonio, I'll be there."

"Then that will be forever, *mi amor,* because I'll love you forever."

Their lips met, tender and light as a summer breeze.

"Well, now, ain't this right real cozy? Unhand my sister, man. Don't make me hurt you."

Startled they pulled apart; Juan Antonio rose quickly and turned on his heel to face the intruder. Carina tried unsuccessfully to stifle a giggle. Standing in the doorway, hands balled into fists, a huge scowl on his face, her five-foot-seven-inch, one-hundred-forty-pound brother, Jesse, faced six-foot, one-hundred-eighty-pound Juan Antonio. This was rich. She couldn't help herself; she burst out laughing.

Both men turned their gazes toward her; one pinned her with a glare, the other with a smile of approval. She exchanged a gentle and promise-filled look with the latter one but turned to talk to the man with a frown the size of Texas.

"Jesse, this is Juan Antonio."

Before she could finish the introduction, Jesse

stepped forward and landed a swift blow to Juan Antonio's chin, clipping his head backward with force.

"Jesse!" Carina screeched. "Are you *loco?*"

"That's for breaking my sister's heart."

Carina reached for Juan Antonio and guided him to the edge of the desk, pulling his hand away so she could examine his face.

"Oh, your beautiful face," she crooned. "You're going to have a bruise." She turned angrily to Jesse. "Look at what you've done, you *desperado.*"

Juan Antonio caught her fluttering hands and she looked up into eyes bright with merriment. She whirled to look at Jesse, who shrugged his shoulders and shot her a look of wide-eyed innocence. She narrowed her eyes at him and he raised one brow, firmed his lips and said, "Bring it, little sister."

Juan Antonio threw back his head and laughed loudly. She watched Jesse's lips twitch with amusement. Her sense of humor took over and in spite of herself she chuckled. Juan Antonio stood and drew her to his side, one arm protectively around her shoulders. He walked them to the door, where Jesse stood and held out his hand. "I'm taking your sister to meet my mother. After that—" he looked down at Carina, his eyes filled with sheen of purpose "—I'm asking her to marry me. Again." He turned back to Jesse. "With your permission."

Jesse studied the two of them for a few moments then accepted Juan Antonio's handshake. With a silken thread of warning in his voice he spoke. "Don't mess this up, man."

Chapter 19

Juan Antonio hugged his mother tightly. The guilt of how he'd wronged her would not abate any time soon, but her arms felt good around him. He'd poured his heart out in front of Carina, hoping to kill two birds with one stone. She'd cried along with him and his mother. Marcelo had been right. What he hadn't understood was why his mother never explained. Just now, she'd answered his curiosity. One parent should never speak badly about their partner, nor bring a rift between a parent and child. How simple. But her silence had almost ruined his life.

"I'm so sorry, Tonio," she said again. "I wish I'd known. I should have paid better attention."

"All is forgiven, Mom. That is, I hope you've forgiven me."

"There was never anything to forgive, son." She

straightened her top and glanced at Carina. "Now tell me, is this young lady a counselor? Has she instructed you to face your demons?"

When they'd walked through the door at the Citrus Queen, where his mother would spend the next three months before returning east, he'd began immediately to question her and to beg forgiveness. Introductions had skipped his mind.

"Mother, this is Carina Garza, the NAFTA inspector who came to Dad's place and inspected mangoes. I plan to ask her to marry me. I've asked permission from her brother and on the way here she told me I have her mother's blessing. I'm waiting for the perfect moment to ask her."

"The perfect moment will be *when* you ask her, and there's no better time than right now." His mother all but clapped her hands in glee. "But wait. Carina, will you excuse us a moment?"

Carina nodded, and watched as the man she loved followed his mother's quick race from the room.

Moments later he returned and crossed to her side. "Come with me, please?" He took her hand and they walked down a hallway to a room at the back of the hacienda. Windows lined the back wall; the room was bright and cheery. Juan Antonio faced her and dropped to his knee. He took her hand, looked into her eyes and asked, "Will you marry me, Carina, and make me the happiest man on earth? I will cherish you till the day I die. You can even work and I'll stay home with the babies. Please?"

"Yes, I'll marry you. But I stay home with the babies." Then she gasped as he slid the most beautiful diamond ring onto her finger.

"My mother just gave this to me. It would please us both if you'd accept it but if you'd rather have one of your own choice, I will be so happy to get it for you."

She pulled him to his feet. "Would you just hurry and kiss me. I've waited so long."

"Ah, *mi amor,* so have I, so have I. But there's one more thing you must look at first." He shook his head at Carina's protest. He turned her to see the wall behind her. A mural of the hacienda in Mexico surrounded by mango trees covered the entire wall. Breathtaking in its beauty, she felt transported back to the place they'd fallen in love. Her eyes widened in delight and she turned to tell him her thoughts. His head descended, his mouth claimed hers with a hunger that shattered her outward calm. She was home.

* * * * *